Heart

~ of the ~

Earth

Robin Craig Clark

HEART OF THE EARTH

Peliguin Publications

Peliguin Publications

books@peliguin.com
peliguin.com

Download Map of Nemeton
Limited Time Only
Visit: peliguin.com

Heart of the Earth
ISBN 978-0-6453716-1-1

For all creatures, great and small.

'In no fix'd place the happy souls reside.
In groves we live, and lie on mossy beds,
By crystal streams, that murmur thro' the meads:
But pass yon easy hill, and thence descend;
The path conducts you to your journey's end.'
This said, he led them up the mountain's brow,
And shews them all the shining fields below.
They wind the hill, and thro' the blissful meadows go.

Publius Vergilius Maro

Chapters

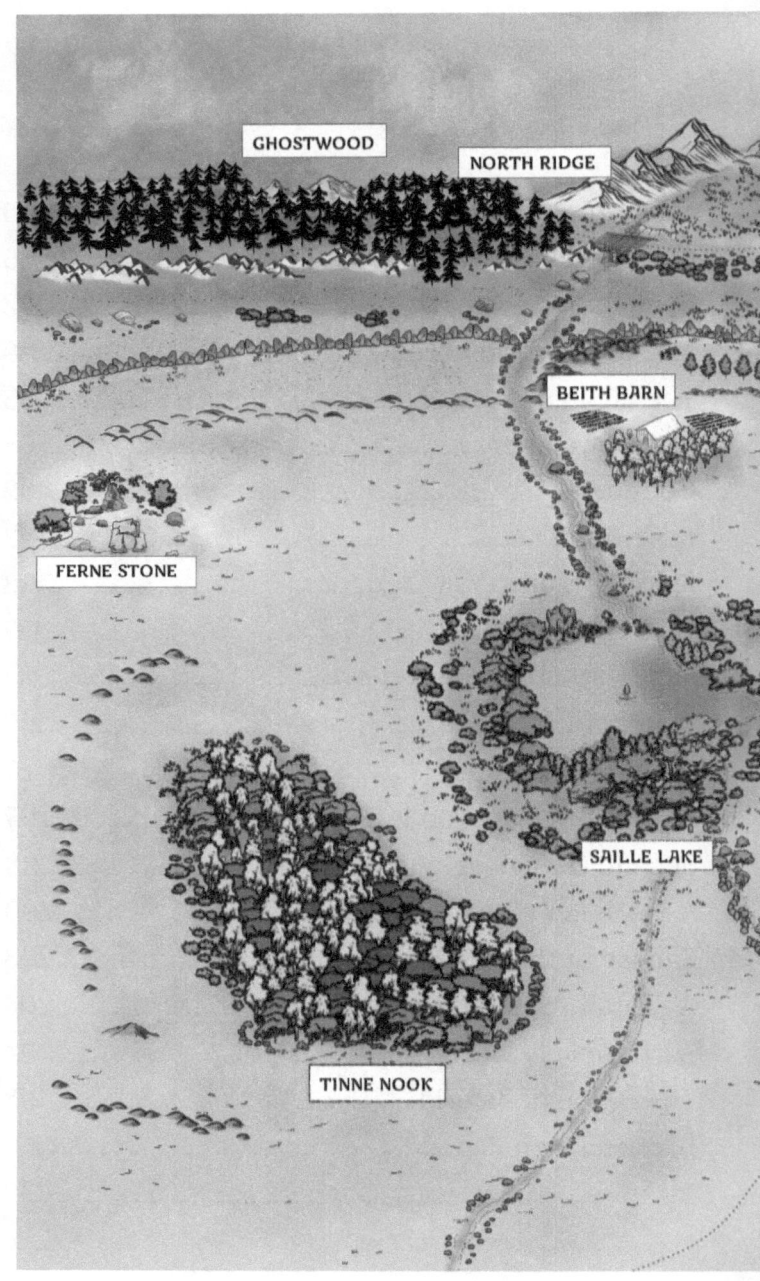

EASTERN RISE

MUIN LANE

HOPE HOUSE

NEMETON

0   1

One Mile

Nemeton

Sofia Deer was crying. Her leg was trapped in the serrated jaws of a deadly gin trap—a *bonebreaker* as it was known throughout the animal kingdom. Struggling only made it worse, tearing to the bone.

The sun began its long gradual descent, the hours passed, and her cries grew feebler. Although each breath became shallower, her heart beat fiercely, holding on to precious life. But she knew the time was nearing, that soon she must prepare to yield and accept the releasing of her spirit. She would embrace her fate and, laying down, rested her head on a clump of cool grass. Surrendering to the act of stillness, there came a deep sense of peace. In the silence of the woodlands, Sofia opened herself up to a greater knowing that her true nature, her real place of belonging, lay not in physical form. Not in the woods and fields. There came a light, emanating from every shimmering leaf and blade of grass. Gazing upward, the sky grew brighter ... indeed, her body, her very being, filled with light. Though her leg was trapped, she knew it was fear that was the true shackle binding her to suffering. Seeing the light in all things, Sofia realised that every life form was an expression, the manifestation of the same light. She was not a body separate from the woods and fields, she was the holy earth upon which she lay, the sacred sky above, the wind blowing gently through the leaves. The universal river of life was flowing from one eternal fountain, and she was returning to that fountain. Sofia closed her eyes, knowing her grasping to life was futile. She *was* LIFE!

By dawn, her body lay motionless. But the young roe deer did not die by the hand of a poacher for she was already liberated, had already returned home to the silent stillness of her origin—the one cosmic light that is never born and never dies.

The woodlands and meadows stood unusually quiet. The rest of the animals of Nemeton, unaware of their provincial connection with the earth, of their true sacred place in the world, quietly mourned another senseless killing, another pointless death. Another *stealing*.

A gentle green giant stood by the shores of Saille Lake, her graceful long fingers reaching down to the water. The wind harped softly through the willow's slender branches where sat a little owl, silent and watchful. Stretching his wing, the owl began to preen, sinking his beak deep into his pied plumage. A downy feather lifted on the wind before resting gently down on the lake. Like a fairy boat spun from fine white silk, the upcurled feather sailed smoothly across the water.

On the windward shore, banked with tall reed beds, a thick green plant of marsh-marigold bore two strange golden flowers. The eyes of a young fox peeked cautiously through the rush grass. Above his shiny red muzzle, his amber-red eyes blazed with intense brightness. The fox stood, poised, watching with fierce attention the owl feather gliding towards him. A leaping fish disturbed the water, and the feather was gone.

Beyond the hidden vale, out beneath wide rolling hills, nestled a small hamlet of cottages and from redbrick chimneys, the curl of rising smoke drifted up to a glowing sky. On the highest hill along the eastern rise, Nemeton church chimed the evening hour. From the spire of that hallowed tower, a weathervane turned on the changing wind, reflecting the last rays of the setting sun.

Along the north ridge, a great pine forest stood, shadowing the landscape. Crows were gathering on the wing, wheeling above the treetops in preparation to roost. *Caw, caw, caw*, the birds cried. One by one they spiralled down; their black bodies vanishing beneath the folds of darkness.

As the moon began its steady climb above the treetops, a path of light reflected across the lake where a shoal of minnow broke the water in a dancing display of synchronicity; their tiny silver scales twinkled like the stars above. Crouching on a lily pad close by the reed bed, a lonesome frog began to croak its evening chant. And somewhere on the far shore, the song of a nightingale filled the air.

Kweeo, kweeo, fluted the owl from the willow tree, and the lake fell silent. Anam Little Owl blinked his bright yellow eyes, cocked his head, then promptly took to the air.

Call of The Wild

eter Goodhope tried to fit in. He made all attempts to live an ordinary life in accordance with the traditions and expectations of the social system. He attained an art degree; worked hard at his job. Pursued a romantic relationship. But deep down, he felt a lacking. Something missing. A space that could never be filled.

His one prized possession was a small green sports car. With its low rounded body and two prominent headlamps mounted above a smile-shaped grill, he named the Austin-Healey Mr Toad, becoming the only motorcar he ever owned and vowed he would keep forever—'Till death do us part'.

Peter read the road sign for Nemeton and turned off the motorway. In the rear-view mirror, he watched the winking lights of a world he was leaving behind. *As one dream fades, another begins*, were his departing thoughts as the city lights blinked out of view. Switching on the radio, Vivaldi's 'Autumn' concerto played from the loudspeaker—violins and orchestra depicting harvest time. He pushed down on the accelerator and gathered speed.

Peter was a master of pen and ink, a painter of fairy-tale landscapes. Secret forests, hidden valleys and cloud-covered mountains became inhabited with animals he'd known as a child—earth angels, he called them; badgers under moonlight, hares in the fields at dawn, foxes posturing on the evening hills— human-like in their pose, bringing a magical realism to his work. He often sketched and painted through the night, when all the world was sleeping, conjuring up wondrous worlds drawn from the cauldron of childhood memories.

Peter's work was much in demand from the many publishers and playhouses across the city. His drawings, paintings and designs often appeared in books and theatre productions. One consignment was for an architectural rendering to the entrance of the city library, his most praised work; a building adorned with 'angels'.

But city life had come to a close. An inheritance brought a new direction. Home would be a house nestled in the quiet vales of the countryside—a place that first captivated his childhood imagination and still held happy and poignant memories of his early years. The time had come for him to write and illustrate his own work. It would be a storybook filled with lore and legend, set in a world of wonder and enchantment, populated by all the magical creatures he'd known as a young boy.

A sleepy violin now played from the speaker as he drove deeper into the night.

It was on the day before Peter's sixth birthday, a dark winter evening, that his parents died. They were returning home after visiting friends when their car struck a patch of black ice and careened off the road. Peter held few memories of their short time spent together, remembering more their voices than their faces. Even now, when trouble called, he would hear their comforting words: *It's okay, Peter. We're right here; you are safe. Everything will be alright.*

His grandparents were kind and provided him a safe and protected life where he spent his formative years at Hope House, their home in Nemeton. The magnificent cedar that grew beside the house was the first tree to speak to Peter. It happened on the morning his grandmother told him of the tragic news. Young Peter was out standing beneath its shade looking up through the long level branches, imagining it to be a stairway to the sky. *What troubles come, can be overcome*, the wind made the leaves sigh. From that day, every afternoon after school, he would seek solace with the cedar, climbing its wooden rungs to reach the conic crown and sit unseen among the fragrant leaves. It was the safest place in the world. There he would look out on wide vistas, dreaming of daring and dangerous adventures, of one day embarking on a journey across those wide-open plains where wood and meadow beckoned him.

Turning seven, Peter discovered his passion for drawing. Grandmother had gifted him with a handmade quill pen with glass holder, a small ink bottle and a sketchpad.

'It's a pheasant's primary flight feather, moulted

from the left wing,' said his grandmother. 'It makes a perfect pen.' The boy gaped at the quill. Holding it, he marvelled how the feather curved gracefully over the back of his hand. He loved the sheen of its russet-brown markings. Adored its unique practicality. Off he raced, into the garden, relentlessly sketching every flower he could find: sweet peas, roses, cornflowers, poppies, zinnias, larkspurs, hollyhocks and dahlias. He filled up the entire sketchpad in a week!

From there, he began studying every bird and beast that frequented Hope House. He would sit under the shade of the apple tree, drawing all that dwelt in the garden. Blackbird and thrush, robin and wren were his daily visitors. He sketched rabbits at dusk, hares at dawn, and on cold nights nearing wintertime, painted fine portraits of hedgehogs he attracted to the grounds with saucers of milk placed on the doorstep. Once, deep in the night, a loud clanging woke him and, standing on the toy box looking down from the bedroom window, he glimpsed his first fox disturbing the dustbins. A whole other world of wonder existed right there in his own backyard.

By the age of nine he could no longer hold back the urge to begin his wilder adventures, and one spring morning, equipped with pen and pad, young Peter climbed the wicker fence and made off across the open fields. Throughout the summer he pencilled and painted the greater landscape, discovered new trees; drew the rowan, the alder and the yew, learnt to identify each through shapes and patterns of leaves, their girders and crowns. He came to know the oak and the ash, sycamore and beech, detailing their seasonal fruits, studying and sketching their seeds and flowers.

It was the quiet groves he loved to wander the most, embracing the silence and solitude; there befriending woodpecker and warbler, the nightingale and nuthatch. Frequent meetings with the owls of the woods allowed him to identify their different body shapes, their feather markings and facial discs, and even from great distances, he came to recognise their notable calls.

Peter would set his easel down by the shores of Saille Lake and paint for hours at a time. He'd observe the changing play of light and shadow, the patterns of trees and clouds reflecting on the water, right down to tiny brushstrokes capturing every ring of water made by carp and minnow.

When reposing on the sedge banks, he often caught a glimpse of a wild animal in its natural habitat. He'd watch them creep and crawl from burrow or nest—one day a badger, the next an otter or stoat would cross his path—all recorded down on paper, drawn with a steady hand.

Other times he would write short stories around the animals he came to know—friends of the forest, he would call them. They became larger-than-life characters; some appointed with magical powers and could talk to one another.

In the autumn of Peter's tenth year was when his grandfather passed away, leaving him and his grandmother to fend for themselves at Hope House. They bonded closer together and became inseparable friends. He enjoyed her sprightly company as much as she did his youthful spirit. Packing picnics of bread and jam and blackberry tea, they easily spent a whole day exploring the untamed landscape.

Above all, Peter enjoyed times of solitariness among the woods. For it was here in such silent and secluded places that nature became his constant companion, inspiring him to become the artist he was today.

Quiet independence and gentle rebellion developed and he would often skip school to be among the flora and fauna; nature's finest seminary—'For what can be gleaned from having your head stuck inside a book without first experiencing the real world?' he argued. Relying not on rote learning but by impressions of nature, his mind was set to be an artist.

On his eighteenth birthday, there came a turning point. Ambitious and self-reliant, Peter left Hope House for life in the city. His Great-Uncle Jack provided him with a small apartment above a coffee shop from where he could earn a wage and pay his way through art college. The day of his departure, leaving Nemeton, marked the beginning of his passage from youth to manhood.

It was on that dreary day, upon hearing the shrill whistle and feeling the sudden jolt of the train as it heaved from the station, his heart sank, leaving a hollowness in his chest. He would never forget sitting in the lonesome carriage holding on to Grandfather's portmanteau, his prized leather suitcase, rubbed and battered from worldly travels. Young Peter clutched tightly to that dear case as though it possessed some supernatural power—so long as he remained holding the braided handles, it provided a charm of protection, giving him courage to face the vast unknown world awaiting him. From the carriage window, he watched his grandmother wave goodbye, standing all alone at the end of the platform.

'Goodbye, Peter, be sure to visit soon,' she shouted over the sound of wheels rolling away on the tracks.

Having bade farewell to Grandmother, leaving his birthplace behind, such a poignant memory would continue to linger and haunt his mind, bringing about an invariable longing to his heart.

Ten years had passed since his departure. Having endured the constant drum of city life, suffering the confined space living above the coffee house, Peter felt free again, eager to return home to Nemeton, his mind brimming with wondrous thoughts of new adventures back in the world he left behind.

The Allegro continued on the radio; solo strings

of violin now imitative of a hunt—the resounding horn and hunted hare, of guns and dogs. Peter turned up the volume, conducting the concerto over the steering wheel as he navigated the winding lanes, passing through village and green, over bridge and stream, enjoying the freedom of the open road. Shifting down a gear, he entered a sharp bend and, reaching the apex of the corner, accelerated in a thrilling squeal of tyres. Another sign for Nemeton and he veered at a left turn, making for another fast curve. The trees and hedgerows whipped by in a steady blur.

Vivaldi's 'Autumn' neared its climax—violins depicting the hunter's pursuit and the panic of prey before its capture. It was at that musical moment between hunter and beast, from out of the dark, a cock pheasant dashed across the road. Peter slammed on the brakes, turning the car to avoid hitting the bird, sending tyres screaming over the asphalt as the car careened out of control. A front wheel mounted the grass verge, striking out a post from the ground. A headlamp blew, its glass lens shattering when the car came to a sudden halt. Peter lunged forward. He could hear the pheasant's far-carrying cry, *Cak-cak-cak-cak*, as it took flight, fleeing into scrub on the far side of the road.

Vivaldi's violin played out its last note, which harried and died as Peter heaved back in his seat with a heavy sigh. He sat staring through the windscreen at a metal post pushed out of the ground. The warning sign read: CAUTION: BLIND CORNER. Did the pheasant just pre-warn him of that perilous bend up ahead? Had the bird not appeared across his path at that given moment, might his fate have been a tragic one? He could still hear the fowl's distressed cries issuing from the dark. Switching off the radio, he started the engine and carefully manoeuvred the car back on the road.

Peter had packed himself a change of clothes and basic food supplies, including his cherished pulverised coffee, a tin of black tea, a tub of honey and a large bag of oats; porridge he could eat any time, day or night. And then there was the bottle of Laphroaig, his most favoured single malt whisky, also not limited to time of day. His surplus needs, all he had acquired over the past ten years, was back in the city, stored provisionally in packing boxes, to be delivered in the morning by the removalists. His one true friend was back there too, living under the glitter of bright lights, choosing to follow her dream of being an actress on the stage.

Peter stopped at a crossroads. There appeared no sign to direct him. He looked lost, uncertain which of three ways would take him home. On the passenger seat sat the portmanteau. Like a charm, the mere touch of the handle was enough to invoke its protective power. He took a deep breath and over the soft purr of the engine came a sudden stir, a gust of wind roaring through the trees behind him. The wind carried over the car, moving through the treetops bearing left down the road, as if to guide him in that direction. Peter engaged the gears and followed the airstream.

The roads became narrower, single lane. Over a packhorse bridge then up a steep hill to where the lane meandered out along a narrow rise. Below, nestled in the valley, tiny lights from cottage windows glowed in the dark.

Having settled into college life, though an unwilling city dweller, Peter constantly yearned for the silence and stillness of nature and would oftentimes visit Nemeton during his summer and winter semesters. Upon each return he observed Grandmother growing ever more frail in her body, though her spirit remained strong. It was becoming evident Grandmother was unable to maintain Hope House on her own, and so it was agreed, though reluctantly on her part, that she would move nearer to the city, under nursing care, to be closer to Peter.

Grandmother never considered selling the property and would not agree to leasing it either. Coverings were placed over the furniture and, with drapes drawn and latches locked, the house lay dormant.

Peter was able to visit Grandmother on a regular basis, which he did faithfully every Sunday for six years until she died peacefully while holding his hand.

Inheritance was not the reason for Peter's return to Nemeton. At first, he planned to auction the house; with Grandmother gone it seemed to no longer play any part in his life. But a voice stirred deep within. Something urged him home. Was it the song of the four winds among the trees? Perhaps the steady babbling, the laughter of water running through the valley? Or maybe the wild animals themselves were calling him. One thing was sure, he felt compelled to recapture glimpses of long-ago forgotten places, those halcyon days of childhood that had first inspired him to become an artist.

On the gatepost at Hope House, Anam Little Owl sat watchful as Peter drove up the gravelled driveway. Anam turned his head, tracking the car's single headlamp as it passed through the open gates, illuminating a row of maples bordering the driveway.

Peter parked beneath the cedar growing by the house. Marvelling at the tree brought memories flooding back of climbing its cross-hatch branches reaching to the sky.

'We made it, Mr Toad.' He breathed a sigh of relief, patting the steering wheel. Turning off the engine he leant back in the seat, staring at the house through the dust swirling in the headlight. So many years had passed. So many memories laid to rest in that old slumbering house. The grounds looked tidy, maintained regularly by Old Tod, the gardener, but nobody had crossed the threshold of Hope House since its doors were locked six years ago. He leaned forward, crossing his arms over the steering wheel. It was in that moment of quiet reflection there came a soft cry of an owl and Peter glimpsed the night bird sweep low across the ground in front of him then rise up over the roof.

Ki-eew, Anam called out.

In the fields beyond the wicker fence, a shadow of an animal came slinking through the tall grass. Lifting its head and with ears pushed forward, the fox scented the air and gave a shrill bark.

Stepping from the car, Peter looked out to where he'd heard the fox. How bright the moon yet dark the sky, where all the fields, trees and hedges had all but melded into one formless expanse. Along the horizon under moonlight, a row of sycamores stuck out against the firmament, like gigantic sentinels guarding the landscape. Amidst the shapeless woods and fields, the moon glistened upon the lake. Again, somewhere among crag and hill, came the gekkering of a fox, followed by the short plaintive cry of an owl.

Retrieving his case from the car, Peter walked up to the house. Above the stone steps the oak door hung, weathered by time. He remembered the tree motif carved into the centre panel of the door and ran his fingers lightly over the notched words: *Hope House*. Above the carving was the same brass figure of a fox, its brush used as a knocker, smoothed and tarnished by the many hands that had clasped it. Taking out a key from his jacket pocket, he turned the cumbrous lock and lifted the latch. The iron hinges groaned as the door yielded slowly to the push. A rich aroma of oak and blackberry issued from the house. He was home.

EnchanTed Land

eter woke with the dawn. Lying next to the fireside on the tufted sofa he watched the last remains of a log collapse into the glowing ash. He got up and put on his scally cap and gazed about the dim room. Grandmother's furniture stood veiled under large white sheets, giving no distinguishable outlines as to what lay beneath. He lifted the first covering, revealing a wooden serving dresser with brass scalloped handles. A pair of crewel-work wing-back chairs were next uncovered facing the hearth. Along the east wall, a rosewood bookcase was unveiled containing Grandmother's library of books. Peter's face lit up seeing those old familiar volumes after so many years: *The Ogham Tree Alphabet, Orbis Arbour, Language of the Ancient Earth*. He ran his fingers gently across their scuffed spines, coming to rest on one leather-bound, timeworn tome—*The Battle of Balor*—embossed in gold lettering. Taking up the book, he leafed through the fusty pages, happy at once to be reunited with a long-forgotten friend. It was his most favourite story, read over and over as a child, ever captivated by the mythical tales of a hideous giant wreaking havoc and destruction upon the land. There were engravings and lithographs used throughout the book, depicting the giant's odious eye centred in its forehead that, when awakened, brought death and destruction to any living thing caught in its gaze. Hideously adorable! He smiled, closed the book and placed it next to *The Ogham Tree Alphabet*.

Removing the next cover, he found a longcase clock standing against the wall by the hallway, its bonnet decorated with woodland motifs and floral meanders. The lower part of the case showed an owl carved into the wood—an image indelibly burned into his mind since a child. He pulled on one of the rose-flower designs, opening a secret drawer that housed a small key. Winding up the three weights he sent the big brass pendulum swinging, steady as a heartbeat. He checked his watch—the timepiece was out by a mere nine minutes. Opening the dial face, he adjusted the hand accordingly.

In the alcove of a large bay window, Peter pulled away the last remaining dustsheet. There in all its grandeur stood Grandfather's mahogany writing desk, with its tooled green leather top and gilt-edging. On the desk sat his 'Good Companion', a 1932 Imperial typewriter, untouched by dust nor aged with time. He pressed the spacebar and the carriage shunted, breathing life into the handsome machine.

He threw open the rose-red drapes that for six years had shut out the light. The bay window offered pleasant views north and east. In the soft dawn light he could see the row of distant sycamores, their graphite shapes emerging through the grey mist like pencilled drawings traced across a paper-white sky. Vapours came rolling off the north ridge where the tall pine forest rose up into low morning cloud. Somewhere he could hear crows cawing on the wing. Looking eastward, the valley lay in shadow, for the sun had not yet risen above the rise. The church stood stark against the bare hills.

Peter turned from the window and considered the position of the desk; the fact it faced into the room bothered him. He rolled the swivel chair aside and, taking a firm hold, pushed the desk around to face the window. From the portmanteau, he took out his pens and inks, paints and brushes, and laid them out in orderly rows alongside the typewriter. With the chair repositioned, he sat with uninterrupted views of the countryside; a perfect place to paint and begin writing his book.

Opening the desk drawer, he found inside a ream of paper. In the lower drawer were three pheasant quills, a penknife for sharpening the tips, a bottle of oak gall ink and a sealed box containing typewriter ribbon, most likely all put there by his grandmother, perhaps knowing that one day he would return. He smiled and then laid the quills next to his own pens. Opening the spools, he installed the ribbon and inserting a sheet of foolscap paper, fed it round the rubber platen. Peter stretched out his arms and flexed his fingers, as if to call up some latent power in his hands. Focusing on the keytop he began to type, rather clumsily. Turning the platen knob, the printed words rolled above the type guide:

HEART OF THE EARTH
By P. J. Goodhope

He leaned back as he pondered the title. Next would come the hard task of finding inspiration. The breath and blood of a writer.

For a while he just sat and stared out of the window, up at the north ridge, then glanced across to the eastern rise, casting his eye over woods and fields that begged to be explored. He rose from the desk and walked out to the hallway.

Putting on his coat, Peter picked up the shillelagh—a blackthorn walking stick that hung at the entrance of the house. The old cane belonged to Grandmother. He remembered her carrying it every time they took their long walks together.

'To make a shillelagh,' she once told him, 'you take a blackthorn root and smear it with butter then shove it up the chimney to cure! That's what turns it black and shiny.' Peter ran his hand reflectively over the bulbous handle, remembering her words clearly. 'The knobble on the end makes a good cudgel if ever the need arises!' How he had laughed when she made a few quick turns, wielding the stick about her like a sword.

Peter buttoned his coat and stepped out into the morning light. He strolled through the open gates, down onto the lane, and started off for those long-ago forgotten places.

From the mist rolling down the hillside, water droplets collected on his face as he crossed a narrow bridge that spanned a small brook. Beyond the bridge stood a century-old waypost heavily encrusted with flakes of lichen, pointing off to a footpath that cut across the western side of Hope Land. Alder and ash trees, having knitted so tightly together, formed a thick hedge that overhung the path. Following the wet track along the edge of the field, his boots soon became caked in clay.

Midway, the path began to slope, leading down to a slow-moving stream flanked with ragwort, dock and nettle. Peter cleaned his boots in the shallows and, sitting beneath a rowan tree growing on the bank, watched a scattering of autumn leaves floating downstream on the lazy current. Looking up through the branches at the harvest of bright red berries, from a gentle stirring of leaves he heard the rowan whisper: *Life is beautiful, life is good.*

An aspen had fallen between the riverbanks, creating a natural bridge. Peter stood and stepped up onto the horizontal trunk and carefully made his way over the stream. On the other side stood Dair Grove, shrouded in mist. Sunrays filtered through the interstices of the trees and there was a small path leading up to the woods where two elms grew on either side forming a Gothic arch of green. To Peter, the woodland had always bestowed a sense of sanctity, a place of peace and refuge, offering any wayfarer shade and shelter from the world outside.

Stepping into the grove, all was silent but for the gentle rustling of an oak. Again, he heard a whispering: *Welcome,* said the oak, *there is magic here, and mystery.* Looking around, many youthful birch trees, 'ladies of the woods', shared proximity with hawthorn and ash. Spread out in more open spaces, the strong and noble oaks grew broad and tall. There came a chattering across the whole canopy—the sound of the wind moving through the top branches. Peter knew at different times of the year the tree's utterances would change. If the north wind did blow, they would moan and thrash their limbs. The east wind brought rejoicing among the trees, and on mid-summer mornings they murmured quietly among themselves with placid motion. Boughs and branches whistled in wintertime where came the song of the south, speaking of the foam-flecked waves that beat incessantly on some distant shore— at such times, the great southern wind would carry the scent of the sea even out into the woods. And the sweet westerly breeze? She made the trees sing soft lullabies every evening as the sun dipped beneath the vale.

Plucking a leaf from the oak and studying its unique lobed form invoked in him the spirit of the carefree wanderer of the woods. How long it had been since he visited the grove. He pressed the leaf to his mouth, breathed in its earthy scent, recalling quiet days sitting under the oak's summer shade with pen and paper. Pushing his face against the rugged bark, he hugged the tree and heard the old oak creak, as if to say, I *remember you.*

He picked another leaf, this time from the ash, noticing how it bore resemblance to a flame—its jagged serrated margins finished with a red-orange tip. Another leaf, a nearby hawthorn, shared a common similarity to both leaves in shape and colour. Peter observed a semblance with the leaves, an underlying pattern, yet each leaf expressed that pattern its own unique way in form and flush. The stalk, midrib and lateral veins of each leaf appeared a miniature image of the tree. The arterial network of interconnecting veins reminded him also of a waterway, where brooks flowed into streams and into larger streams, tributaries converging into one main river. He had seen this same fluting outline elsewhere, in the delicate wing markings of a butterfly, a dragonfly, the humble honeybee. The image reminded him also of the teaching from the Tree of Life. That all things are connected and related. Could this simple pattern found in a leaf be a common theme that binds all the world with nature? Was it nature's grand design for regeneration and immortality? He spread the leaves over a large obtruding root and from his jacket pocket took out his pencil and pad and began sketching his findings.

After slipping the pencil back into his pocket, with the soft light pushing through the mist, he went brushing through the fallen leaves, and the spicy smells of wet woods recalled in him another disowned memory, a joy half-forgotten, when as a boy he had lain beneath the sycamores studying their samaras; pairs of winged fruit that would spontaneously detach from the tree at spirited random; spinning and spiralling to earth; some carrying far and wide on the wind. And here in the grove—that same primal feeling, a knowing that everything in nature is utterly and unshakably in harmony and balance. All connecting. All originating from the one flowing fountain of life.

There came reconciliation. Peter felt a deep peace, found again his bliss. No more the grim ineffable hollowness yawned in his chest, but joy and belonging.

Clambering over a fallen tree laying across the woodland path, a startled pigeon rose up from the ground, wings whipping into a power-lift as she fled to a far distant region. It was then Peter noticed a well-worn path marked by badgers. Following their tracks between the bracken, the ground sloped smoothly down to a sandy shore. There, in all its serene beauty, was Saille Lake. In a momentary daze, Peter stood looking out upon his childhood haven, marvelling at the mist whirling a ghostly dance over

31

the tranquil water.

As a child the lake had always seemed so immense, unfathomable, stretching as long as it was wide; a vast ocean impossible to cross. Now the mere appeared so much smaller—a modest green pool hidden among the trees. But still beautiful, still as mysterious as he remembered.

Peter walked close to the shore where wavelets lapped gently between the reed mace. Standing at the water's edge he raised his head and, with open arms, breathed in the delicious bucolic air; the fragrance of autumn, of wet twigs, damp leaves and oakmoss. Hedging the bank, bulrushes poked up their velvety heads, some having split to scatter their seeds. There came scuttling between the sedge grass and Peter caught a glimpse of bronzed fur and webbed paw as a pair of otters slipped silently into the water, leaving barely a ripple.

Above the veiled treetops came the rising whir of wings and, with weary cries, a flock of greylag geese, their long necks pushed forward, appeared through the misty sky. Peter watched the skein turn in perfect formation, their wings beating in unison as they passed over the lake, calling one to the other to follow in a new direction.

On the eastern shore, Anam Little Owl sat reposing, swathed in the willow's gentle arms, listening to the lilting leaves and the quiet rippling of water. His eyes grew heavy with sleep, half closing when, at once, he startled to the sound of a footfall, gentle and soft upon the earth. A human stepped up beneath the tree just below his perch. Anam watched with lively curiosity as the figure moved along the shoreline, kicking idly through the wet shale.

Picking up a pebble, Peter sent the stone skipping across the water, watching it disappear into a cloud of mist that hugged the lake. With the first blush of morning sun, shafts of light fell aslant between the trees and Peter stood in awe of dawn's creation. As he stood there, gazing on the water, watching the mist gradually lift, a wraithlike shape appeared on the lake just where he had cast the stone. The form seemed no more than four feet high, standing up from the level of the water. As the mist slowly dissipated, so the shape became more distinct; thicker at the base, becoming thinner before tapering to a point. With eyes straining, Peter stepped closer to the shore, his boots touching the waterline. The apparition looked like the hilt and blade of a great sword rising out from the lake.

The warming sun absorbed the last of the water droplets in a swirling, gyrating display, and at last he could see the form clearly—it was an arbour vitae, a young thuja tree, growing on a small rocky isle out in the centre of the lake. He laughed to himself, amused at how his mind had so readily conjured up an old boyish fancy.

Just then a moorhen came gliding through the water, trailing her brood behind. Peter stood a moment to watch the hen and chicks scuttle up onto the small rocky island, promptly sitting beneath the little tree. With the sun shining on the western shore, a crowd of rowdy ravens fluttered about the crown of a large beech. He listened to their noisy banter as they took to the air.

From his secret perch, Anam observed the human making off along the shoreline. Taking leave of the willow, he went skittering along the water's edge, as if to follow.

Peter came to a small stream that had carved rills and crevices into the hillside before coursing into the lake. Using the shillelagh walking stick to steady him, he climbed the slippery knoll and at length came up onto wide-open farmland. Ploughed fields stretched to some illimitable distance beneath white flocks of cloud and where the cumulus parted came intermittent rays of sunshine spotting the landscape.

Bounded on three sides by birch trees stood a long wooden structure—Beith Barn. It had been one of Peter's favourite haunts as a boy, a perfect hideout where he could practice shooting his break barrel rifle Grandfather had entrusted him on his ninth birthday. The smooth feel of that deep-blue barrel and walnut stock balanced in the shoulder held a lasting memory. He recalled his grandfather teaching him how to hold the gun.

'It's all about the lock and load,' said his grandfather. 'The careful aim, the ease of trigger, the resounding ring that marks a hit.' An assortment of old glass bottles, jars and tins were lined along the back wall of the barn and pelted with .22 pellets. His childish curiosity for shooting was quelled simply by firing at the inanimate targets.

The ravages of time had been harsh on the old cruck barn, which had now fallen into disrepair.

Parts of the outer walls were collapsing, leaving remnants of clay and limestone rubble around the cobbled footings. The barn doors had long gone, replaced by a curtain of cobweb. Peter peered gingerly through the thick silky strands. The sun beamed down through a hole in the thatch, bathing the barn floor in a pool of morning light.

Brushing apart the gangly web, Peter entered the barn. At first, he did not notice the owl sitting there, perched on one of the tie beams high in the roof. With keen interest, Anam gazed down through the dust-speckled sunlight.

The interior of the barn resembled a cathedral with its complexity of oak arches soaring overhead. Pairs of naturally curved timbers reached up to the roof and the walls were interlaced with wooden staves. Scattered on the floor lay several hay rakes and forks. A dyke shovel and besom stood upright inside an oaken seed bucket. There were chaff cutters, sickles, an old scythe and reaping hooks hanging from chains on the upright posts. By an old harrow, part of a horse plough propped up a hay cart that long ago had suffered a broken wheel and was now serving as a nesting place for field mice, which darted about in all directions.

Peter began walking round the barn, running his hands across the trappings and tackle and began to imagine how his ancestors had once lived: men clothed in breeches and smocks, women in bonnets and frocks, toiling the arable land. Bearded faces sweating under wide-brimmed hats, pushing the plough through the rich earth. He envisioned brawny lads broadcasting the seeds, scything wheat, threshing and winnowing the harvest grain, and while happy children went running under the noon-time sun, women were at work, raking and forking the hay, others binding the wheat or stooking the sheaves. Pretty maids, also he fancied; their glowing faces and pinkly cheeks, carrying willow baskets brimming with bread and cheese, providing the peasants with flagons of ale.

Peter stood beside an upright post where the reverie of a vanished world faded away. His gaze was now inexplicably drawn to a length of chain where lever binders hung from a wind-brace, and higher up, out on a tie beam among the bate rafters, he spotted the owl. He noted the bird's white and buff barred plumage, its short stoutly body. The flat head, the spray of stubby grey bristles slantwise above the eyes gave a most enduring frown.

'Hello, Little Owl ... I hope I'm not trespassing,' Peter said, smiling up.

Anam took off with a gentle cry, *Kiew, kiew*, flying low over Peter's head, then out of the barn and away across the field. Peter turned, totally enchanted, watching the owl, with its series of rapid wingbeats and looping glides, vanish into a wispy cloud.

The Otherworld

Anam was wide awake, far too excited to sleep. With the sun warming his face, he beat his wings ardently, feeling the wind thrumming through every vane. He was on his way over to see Otus Long-Eared Owl.

It happened one moonless night, while still a baby—Anam's parents went out to gather food, but never returned. Otus Owl, then residing in an abandoned crow's nest at the top of a towering pine nearby, heard Anam's beseeching, his crying out to be fed, and felt it a duty to take care of the woodland foundling. Otus raised the fledgling like one of his own. Winged warrior, master predator, Otus taught

Anam the art of silent flying; how to swoop, how to dive, how to seize prey without a sound.

Anam passed round the south rim of Tinne Nook, a sheltered woodland far from any farmland. He followed the rutted deer tracks and sighted two human fledglings on bicycles. He flew daringly close behind them before cutting off into the quiet shade of the woods, sweeping a wide berth beneath the spreading branches of a horse-chestnut, its wide sweeping branches laden with bright green nut burrs.

With graceful undulations, Anam neared the impenetrable holly bush growing in the middle of the wood and gave a low tactful call, Ki-ew.

Otus Long-Eared Owl lived a reclusive life. Asleep and camouflaged under a bedcover of prickly leaves, he heard Anam's furtive cry. Two orange eyes opened in a flash. He watched Anam come swooping down through the crown of the bush, landing on a branch opposite him.

Folding his wings, Anam wiggled and nodded, and a trill burst from his short, curved beak.

'Lovely day, Otus. Thought I'd drop in, hope I'm not disturbing you?'

The long-eared owl scowled at the little owl.

'Oh, it's you, Anam,' Otus hissed. 'What brings you here this hour of the day? It better be important.' The old owl turned his head, glowering down through the green foliage of his fortress, making sure Anam was quite alone.

Anam rushed to get his words out.

'Otus—a newcomer has arrived on Hope Land, he may be the one Dru Barn Owl predicted was coming.' Anam jiggled with excitement. 'I looked him right in the eye, Otus. I saw gentleness there, and he spoke to me in the human language. He called me "Little Owl"—he knew my name!' Otus glared but said nothing. Anam continued, 'We must visit Dru right away. He will know.' Anam bounced along the bough with unrestrained energy.

Aware of Anam's naivety, Otus looked upon him with a jaded expression.

'Anam, you are very young and very impressionable,' Otus hooted heartlessly. 'You know nothing about prediction or prophecy. You are not a soothsayer, Anam, you are an owl of the woods.'

Anam's enthusiasm quickly drained. He stopped bouncing while Otus maintained his cold and impervious stare.

'You must learn to tame your eagerness, Anam,' said the old owl after a long, restrained silence. 'You see only what your foolish heart hopes for, and now you put yourself and myself at risk by showing off to the newcomer—which, I may add, is old news.' Otus hinged forward on his perch, towering over Anam. 'Sion Fox knows of this stranger, has already put out the warning.' With ear tufts sprung, Otus glared, unblinking. 'You are easy to fool, Anam, and therefore vulnerable to man's ensnaring nature.' Anam's beak swung open, lost for words. Otus looked through the branches out at the woods. 'If news gets around that us owls are hiding here, then not just our parliament but other clans and tribes across the land will be in danger.' Anam's beak snapped shut; all he could furnish was a modest squeak.

Otus cocked his head and gave another scowl of disapproval. 'We feed, we sleep, we live on the wing. That's what we do, Anam. We do not hold power of prophecy; mere mortal owls are we.'

For a few minutes, the two birds considered one another in silence.

Reviving a quiet passion, Anam raised his head.

'But I saw something this time, Otus. Something special shone in his eyes. Something deep inside told me this human was one of a kind.'

'It's nothing but vanities, dreams and shadows,' Otus squawked, snapping his beak angrily. 'Forget such foolish fantasies. Sion has given caution that all animals be on guard, he says this stealer also carries the thunderfire!'

'Thunderfire!' Anam echoed, abhorred by such a statement. He let out several piercing, *Kee-iks*, his petulant cries resonating deep into the woods. Otus ignored the foolish outburst and cast a casual look to the ground. Below them, the two young humans came whipping by on their bicycles, looking up to where the screeching had been heard. One of the boys braked, stopping abruptly beneath the bush.

Otus peered down at the human fledgling before glaring back at Anam. Realising he had attracted undesirable company, Anam's beak trembled as he held his breath. Before the moment could evolve, the two owls simultaneously took to wing, flying off into the sun-dapppled woods.

Reaching the upper boundary of Hope Land, Peter

came to a drystone wall. Using the protruding steps laid within the interlocking stones, he climbed over and stood at the top of Muin Lane. He had walked almost full circle and could see his house at the bottom of the hill, just where the road narrowed over the stone bridge from where he started.

The lane divided two ways at right angles. Looking left, wheel-furrowed tracks ran along the north ridge leading out to Ghostwood—five hundred acres of dense pine trees dominating the landscape. Never once had he ventured into that dark place, not even as a careless child. Seeing the forest recalled aged-old whisperings of tales told. From his earliest recollection, he remembered such idle talk of a hunted murderer that disappeared into that dreadful wood, found later hanging inside the hollow of a tree, long after his bones had been picked by crows. Following the grisly discovery there came rumours of a haunting; stories of sweeping shadows, low, indistinguishable breathings and muffled footsteps, claimed to be that of the dead man still prowling the woods.

'Let it be known that whoever be unfortunate to behold that ghostly figure on a moonless night shall, with cold-curdling scream, vanish without a trace,' came the booming voice of the local innkeeper. Peter remembered himself as a child, cringing on hearing the warning, sitting beneath an open window of the Hare and Hounds public house. The echo of the innkeeper's voice faded leaving only a distant howl of wind cutting through the trees.

Turning from the forest, looking to his right, the lane continued on along the eastern rise where the flint rubble tower of Nemeton church stood grey against the hill. Below the rise, a cluster of cottages, some painted a shade of primrose-yellow, others a deep rose pink or brilliant daisy-white, all nestled in the valley not half a mile away.

He'd finished exploring for the day and started down the lane towards Hope House. With fluting song, Dreean Wren came flitting through the blackberry and hawthorn that bordered one side of the lane. On the opposite side was flat grazing land and home to Spiér Skylark. Rising from the nest, the winged angel soared high above the meadow, filling the sky with her heavenly song. Along with the grasshoppers chirping in the warm grass, the low hum of bees among the clover flowers, and with Merlyn Blackbird and Brych Thrush now accompanying the sweet wren of the lane, such sounds became music to Peter's ears and he joined the minstrels of the meadow, whistling along as he ambled home.

Some way down the lane, between warbles and whistles, there came a deafening thunderclap, yet the sky appeared cloudless, clear and bright. The echo of the blast travelled above the lane and Peter searched the horizon as the thundering boom rolled out along the rise. The roar rumbled and faded, until silence befell the lane.

Arrh! arrh, arrh, came distant cries of rooks as they fled from Ghostwood, clearly disturbed from their roost-trees. Peter watched the band of birds drift languidly from the ridge, moving towards the village above the rise.

A few guarded steps and another crack of thunder, much louder, rending the air as if the sky split open. Looking back over his shoulder, Peter saw a vehicle appear from the direction of Ghostwood, its engine backfiring with great plumes of blue smoke rising out from the tailpipe. It snaked its way along the ridge and Peter lifted a hand to shade his eyes, watching its progress as it approached the top of the lane, stopping by the stone wall. Again, the vehicle backfired, loud as a gunshot, then started down towards him.

Peter mounted the grassy bank, shouldering a hawthorn, as the rickety black van drew up in a squeal of brakes. The door of the van slid open.

'Hello, pilgrim, need a lift?' the driver asked, in a strong Manx accent.

Stepping back onto the lane, Peter sidled up to the open van immediately noticing the man's duck-tailed beard so meticulously waxed and groomed. He wore the finest apparel: a deerstalker hat with red and black houndstooth check, a bright floral tie and twill weave waistcoat, all in stark contrast to the muddy wading boots.

'Good morning,' said Peter, half-smiling.

'Welcome to Nemeton.' The man beamed, poking out his arm. 'The name's Fingal Ollick Morion, but you can call me Morion; I'm the local game-keeper for Herne Estate, managing most of the farm-land and woods up there on the ridge. I keep the pests down for the farmers, stocks up for the hunters.'

Peter noticed the man had a missing forefinger

and at first was reluctant to shake his hand. 'Hello, Morion, I'm Peter Goodhope.' He warmed, and greeted him with a firm grip. 'I've just moved—'

'I know, Mr Goodhope,' interrupted Morion, 'you've recently inherited Hope House from our dear old lady Goodhope—God rest her soul. Such a sad loss.'

Peter measured up Morion, throwing him a side-ways glance. 'How do you know about my—' but again Peter was cut off in mid-sentence.

'You're the old girl's only surviving relative, I believe,' continued Morion. 'Last of a breed. News spreads like weeds round here, Mr Goodhope.' Morion rubbed down his moustache, checking his beard in the side-view mirror. 'We're getting some lovely clear skies for this time of year.' He leaned out of the door, peering up at the sky. 'Though watching those rooks windin' above the rise, I do believe bad weather is on the way.'

The van, with its pug-nose and low open sides fitted with a canvas top, was an old Bedford pickup. The van suffered a dented fender and badly bent bumper, and a headlamp was missing, leaving a gaping hole surrounded by crumpled metal. While

Morion was busy straightening his tie, idly remarking on the changing seasons, something else caught Peter's attention. Down the side of the van, beneath its torn cowling, he observed a vision vaguely familiar—bronzed fur, a webbed paw stained with blood. Peering closer—a dead weasel and a buzzard lay next to the otter and a row of crows, all laid out neatly in small wooden crates, their necks oddly twisted to one side.

Morion caught Peter in the mirror.

With puckered brow, Peter turned.

'Planning to stay long?' enquired Morion, holding a straight face.

Peter quickly gathered his thoughts. 'I've given up my city job,' he said, his voice straining. 'So I could return to Nemeton, the place where I was born. This is my home.' Peter's face had suddenly drained of its morning glow.

'Good for you, Mr Goodhope,' Morion replied with a shy look of guilt. 'Well?' he asked.

'Well, what?' Peter leaned closer, staring him straight in the eye.

Morion was about to remind Peter of his offer of a lift then quickly changed his mind. 'Well ... welcome back to Nemeton, Mr Goodhope.' And without further ado, he ground the gears and drove off in a cloud of smoke.

Peter stood wincing at the trail of fumes left lingering in the lane, watching as the Bedford lumbered down the hill and turning the corner, was lost to sight.

Peter continued on his way. The fields and sky filled again with nature's sweet musicians—and so beautifully coordinated were the singing birds it was hardly possible for him to distinguish them. But then Peter was strangely broody, his mind troubled by what he had seen in the back of Morion's van.

Anam and Otus were on their way to visit Dru Barn Owl, who lived beyond the valley in secluded meadowland far from human habitation. Otus thought it was the thing to do since he would not return to the holly tree until night had befallen Tinne Nook.

Otus had a sharp eye and was a learned flyer and kept Anam close to his wing. He decided they would take the shortcut. What was once known as Ailm Forest had now been renamed Ghostwood, for many a bird and beast had recently disappeared there without a trace. Sinister sightings of humans carrying bonebreakers and thunderfires had been observed of late. Word was out for all animals to stay away from the forest.

The broad sweeping canopies were so thickly ganged it was at times impossible to see the ground from the air. There were thousands of trees stretching for endless miles, yet not a single bird could be heard, nor a creature seen.

'Up here, Ghostwood looks no different to any other wood,' piped Anam, rolling to the right in playful flight, feeling the air rippling under his feathers.

'Don't get any wild ideas, Anam,' squawked Otus. 'That's the forbidden forest. You go in—and you never come out.'

Spellbound, Anam stared down into the blackness below.

The owls safely reached the far side. They left the dark woods behind, banking low over the edge of a steep gully where the ground dropped dramatically into a deep emerald valley. In the distance, with its summit still shrouded in mist, stood Annwyn Mountain, the birthplace of Awen River, where the water starts its long journey down the rocky falls, flowing over the green plains, searching out the sea.

Anam and Otus followed the bends of the bright running river, flying between the grassy hills marked by white dots of grazing sheep, some resting in narrow hollows, others huddling under windswept hawthorn. Down through the valley they flew, onwards to the start of the uplands.

Leaving the river behind, the two owls passed through an avenue of elms shimmering gold against the morning blue. Dru lived close by in the hollow of an ancient oak. For centuries the old tree had stood among flowers of the meadow, pushing its gnarled roots above the ground, reaching out its widening branches, offering sanctuary to any bird or beast.

It happened one winter night—a snow-laden bough became too much for the oak to bear. The bough dropped, leaving a round opening in the bole of the tree. Through cycles of seasons and wood-boring beetles, the sapwood decayed around the cavity, uncovering the heartwood. The hollow dried, making it a homely place for such solitary creatures.

The dead bough still lay beneath the tree, col-onised by fungi, lichen and moss, which over time turned most of the limb to humus, returning it back to the earth. New life sprang up all around the decaying wood; hosts of golden buttercups, a sprinkling of white-moon daisies and a carpet of clover, where happily droned the bumblebees.

Anam and Otus alighted on one of the oak's broad sweeping branches. They sat settling their feathers among the dry flavescent leaves that tinkled in the wind.

The distant church chimed noon just as Peter returned home.

Rooks Removal Company had come and gone, leaving their calling card wedged under the doorknocker. So enchanted had he been by the world of nature, Peter had completely forgotten about the delivery of all his furniture. Having left the house unlocked, he lifted the latch and went inside.

Packing boxes cluttered the hallway. Two artist's easels and numerous canvases were stacked on the kitchen table. In the centre of the lounge lay his walnut bed in three pieces, two bedside cabinets, a dresser and storage drawers. He sighed at the jumble of furniture.

Walking to the bay window, Peter gazed out at the rural scene, quietly reflecting on his morning walk. He made study of the church on the eastern hill. Of Ghostwood overshadowing the north ridge. Watched the rooks winding back from the rise. After a short while, he sat at his desk, loaded the Imperial with a new sheet of paper, and began to type.

The Stealers

Not a mile from Nemeton, down a path choked with nettle, half-hidden within a narrow coomb, stood an old abandoned house, Straif Manor. Grown about with thickets of blackthorn, tenacious ivy had climbed the stone facia, penetrated many of the broken windows, and smothered the roof now in danger of collapsing.

Against the darkening sky, Brân Raven flew with slow pounding wings.

Craark, crark, cr-ark …

North-facing, hemmed in between the hills, the house received modest sunlight in any season. The interior was cast in constant gloom from vines that veiled the windows; dark green foliage dripped from almost permanent wetness, brought in by low cloud that favoured the hollow. The dampness over the years had penetrated the internal walls, staining them black, and mould and mildew flourished on the flagstone floor.

A wooden staircase stood rotten, partly collapsed in a pool of dank water. Doors leaned precariously from their hinges and ceilings bowed, crumbling into piles of plaster to form a sludge on the puddled ground. Every room appeared empty of furnishings, all except one at the very back of the house; the scullery. Dozens of wooden crates were stacked high to the ceiling at one end; a tall metal rack containing various glass bottles and jars took up the rest of the wall. Above two slate sinks hung poachers' paraphernalia; various rabbit nets and rounds of twenty-five-gauge copper wire. A grub axe, spade and billhook hung from a shelf. Two hunting guns—one a rook-rifle, the other a smoothbore—leaned upright inside a copper; a round metal tub. A spring steel device, a gin trap, with grim serrated flanges, dangled down the side of the old wood stove where stood an animal mount—a pair of stuffed carrion crows showing their stout pointed beaks pecking out the eyes of a partridge.

In the middle of the room was a long table where five men sat brooding, dimly lit by a single paraffin lamp. At one end of the board hunched Morion, the gamekeeper, brow beading with sweat, legs jittering nervously under the table. At the opposite end sat Balorid, whose cold callous heart within the man carved out his riven features. He bore a pointed nose, chiselled sharp as flint. Had shrunken cheeks and a lean mouth. He stared at Morion with his one seeing eye, the other hidden under folds of wrinkled skin.

The three other men occupied one length of the table, dressed in camouflage clothing, their aged-old faces smudged with soil. Jonas was the eldest; long and lanky; a pencil moustache grew above his scarred lip. Next to him sat Morgan; a frowsy of white hair sprouted from under his hunting hat. Wild eyes, shaggy beard and a mouth aslant with palsy made him appear the bearer of an idle brain. In contrast, Fenning had no show of hair; smooth-shaven, his prominent low-hanging ears stuck out like amphora handles. None of the men spoke but sat with blank expressions.

Upon the table stood a stuffed weasel, frozen in tense action with bared fangs. Next to it perched a golden eagle, mounted on clay rock with wings out-stretched, its soulless carcass reduced to a mere caricature, bereft of its once full and noble life. Beside the bird of prey, another stuffed animal, a baby badger, her banded head bent, frozen evermore to gaze blindly upon the ground; a mockery of what was once a beautiful and magnificent creature.

Balorid stood—the moving of his chair on the flagstone broke the silence but the grating only made the moment more formidable. Balorid wasn't a tall man, nor muscular—his strength lay in his men-acing demeanour. He walked with the slow deliber-ate gait of a predator stalking its prey. With his one eye fixed determinedly on Morion, he slammed his fist on the table, toppling the weasel.

'Why don't you be more exact, Morion?' Balorid demanded, in a cold imperious voice. 'I get the dis-tinct impression there's something you're not telling us.' His lip arched above his top teeth like a snarling beast about to bite. Morion's head was shaking, mouth agape, noticing Balorid's flaccid eyelid was beginning to convulse, the concertina folds of skin rising, as if pulled up by some invisible string. Morion threw a fitful look at his three comrades. Fenning, Jonas and Morgan sat frozen, statue-like, watching with horror as Balorid's hideous eyelid fully opened. They each turned their heads. But Morion could not avert his gaze, held trancelike by that hideous bulbaceous eyeball.

Dearg was the sixth member of the group. His gaunt face and gangly body appeared at the opening of a wall where once hung a door to the kitchen. His leathery hands dripped with a greyish slime which he wiped down his blood-stained apron. Dearg looked at the men sitting there staring silently into space. Balorid had Morion held in his death-stare. Dearg sniggered, seeming to know what was about to unfold.

Morion shuffled uneasily in his chair, 'I found out today old lady Goodhope's last living relative has decided not to sell Hope House,' he said, his voice trembling, unable to escape Balorid's hypnotic stare. 'We need the thoroughfare for our traps,' he exclaimed. 'There are heaps of pheasants accruing on Hope Land, and I've seen more badgers and owls out there than anywhere else. I spotted a pair of otters down by the lake and managed to trap one earlier this morning.' Morion half-smiled—his mouth was tense. 'I also saw paw marks of a fox down by the lakeside. Animals are becoming scarce elsewhere. Like they're all migrating onto Hope Land.'

Balorid glared while Morion continued, 'This stranger has appeared out of the blue, right in the middle of us setting new traps. Hope House was supposed to go up for auction in a few weeks, which meant we had time to bait the land. Now the old lady's grandson has shown up and decided to keep the house, make it his home.'

Tongue protruding to moisten his limacine lips, Dearg sniggered while he lit a cigarette. He nodded his head with mild amusement.

Morion took a deep breath, half-considering it might be his last. 'I thought it best to introduce myself. I wanted to check him out, find out what his future plans were. I remembered I had fresh quarry laying in crates in the back of the van, so I bid him farewell and drove off.' With pleading eyes, he continued, 'I promise you, Balorid, he saw nothing, knows nothing.' Morion finished his defence, holding a pained smile.

Jonas, Fenning and Morgan kept their heads averted.

Dearg sucked his teeth, blew out a plume of smoke and grinned.

Morion slouched in his chair, somewhat relieved at having justified his actions. With fingers twitching, he smoothed down his moustache. Balorid leaned closer–his monstrous eye staring across the table. Reaching, he took Morion by the necktie and began tightening the knot. Unable to breathe, Morion's face turned a shade of scarlet as he began to choke.

'Morion, Morion, you moron,' said Balorid, wrenching the tie ever tighter. 'You should learn to keep your big trap shut.' And with those words, he dragged Morion across the table, sliding him head-first into a stack of crates that toppled over his body.

'Brain-drain,' said Balorid grimly, turning to Dearg. 'And mount his ugly head in a glass case if you like, as a reminder to the rest of these dismal idiots never to engage with the enemy.'

Dearg laughed, odious and obscene, his tongue whipping side to side. He was delighted. He'd never made a mount from a human head before!

Walking around the table, Balorid's giant eyelid closed as he calmly proceeded with the meeting.

'I have an appointment in the city today,' Balorid announced. 'We're going to span the oceans and reach the four corners of the earth!' He placed the weasel upright to face the three men. 'Our stuffed little critters will be travelling overseas to wealthy aristocrats, wishing to furnish their mansions with our prized trophies. That's the way the money goes.' Raising his thumb and extending his forefinger, he mimicked the shape of a gun, pointing his finger at the back of the animal's head. 'POP! goes the weasel,' he quipped, holding a grim smile. The party laughed nervously at Balorid's rare show of humour.

'Only use rook rifles on Hope Land and shot-guns strictly at night,' said Balorid. 'Absolute top-secret must be maintained to avoid rousing suspicion from the community.' Scowling, he lunged at his minions. 'No one must know who we are, or what we do. Stealth is the secret to our success.' He paced the room. 'Set springs for the owls by the hollows, wires on the rabbit runs. Lay birdlime for small birds, nets for fowls of the field. Use lamping and shoot anything dazzled in your spotlight. Save the gin traps for bigger beasts, for fox and badger, place them at the entrance of every burrow. Take guns to the coverts when hunting pheasant and partridge. Shoot sparingly and not in open fields—keep close to the woods.'

Balorid stood back at the head of the table, his one eye measuring his men.

'Jonas, Fenning, Morgan—it's back to business.' The old men twitched in their chairs, each nodding in unison. 'Go catch me a fox! Or anything furred and feathered.' The three oldsters hurried to their feet. Balorid raised his fist high in the air. 'But no snakes.' His mouth cast downward. 'Nobody likes snakes.'

The Newcomer

Behind a mantle of mistletoe, Dru Barn Owl peered out from his shady hollow. He had eyes of blackest opal and a face as white as snow. Pied plumage of buff and grey shimmered on both his crest and crown. Gold-specked and faintly marked lozenges of deep brown feathers marked the camber of his wings. Dru was a silent watcher; a sound listener; a wise old owl was he.

Perched on neighbouring boughs, Anam and Otus sat imbued with reverence for their elder. A wisp of wind passed between them blowing a single oak leaf from its stem.

Dru looked at Anam then slowly turned to Otus.

There was a long, contemplated moment of silence between the birds.

'You say you know of this newcomer, Otus?' Dru asked. 'Have you also encountered the human?'

Otus stood stern of face, head feathers raised. 'No, Dru, I have not seen the stranger, but have recently heard Sion Fox warning all animals to be on their guard.' His orange eyes widened and glowered. Otus leaned forward on the bough. 'Sion says the stranger carries a stick, most likely a thunderfire, so I expect he is yet another stealer come to torment us.' Otus glanced sideways at Anam, casting him a scornful look.

Dru poked his head further out from the hollow. 'Otus, going by what young Anam has told us, you must also meet with the newcomer. Anam will accompany you, for it will be the first time in owl history that such a meeting takes place.' Dru's face lit up as he leaned further out into the light of day. 'You have to get up close to the newcomer, face to face, look him in the eye, Otus. If he sees himself in you, if he sees the world as you do, then he is Fireun, watcher of the skies, here to free us from our tormentors.' Anam and Otus sat unmoving. 'Through distillation of the spirit,' continued Dru, 'and by refinement of the senses, shall this human enter fully into our world.' The barn owl lent back into shadow. 'When two kindred souls meet, a confluence forms that joins them in an ancient and eternal way. Two become one.' A sudden breeze passed between the birds, shaking many leaves off the tree. Dru leaned out, peering up at the sky. 'I sense Fireun is near.'

Dru recoiled again inside his treehouse. Part in shadow, he turned and looked kindly at Anam. 'If this newcomer proves to be the one, then we all have much to learn, and there will be many dangers to face and difficulties to overcome. Return here in three days.' Dru then gave a loud shriek: 'Go do what you must do!' The old owl withdrew deeper into his wooded cave.

Anam rocked from side to side, giddy with excitement, fuelled by youthful passion. Otus, on the other branch, did not share the same enthusiasm, but only stared coldly at Anam.

The longcase clock whirled and played out its chime. Peter looked up from typing. On the last strike of the clock, it was as though Peter was struck by a flash of insight. Gazing out the window he saw slivers of sunlight glinting on the lake between the trees. Looking northward, circling above Ghostwood, a solitary crow gave out its long lamenting cry. On the hill on the rise, he studied the church marked with the radiance of the setting sun.

Head bent, he struck at the keys for a few more minutes, putting thoughts to paper. Removing the page, he placed it on the desk next to a drawing he had done of a little owl sitting high in the rafters of the old cruck barn.

Inserting a new sheet, Peter sat pondering the blank page. His mind flashed with images of Morion the gamekeeper, his dapper bearded face beaming at him from the van, his wet wading boots and the grimy hand with its missing finger. He recalled the dead otter, the rows of birds, their stiff black bodies, and the uncanny way their heads were twisted in the same direction. The vision startled him, and with suddenness he rose from the chair. Taking leave of his desk, he found relief by the window, gazing out upon the quiet, peaceful grounds.

Looking off at the garden path meandering

under the arbour, his eye rested on the malus tree growing over the wall, its gangly branches loaded with ripened red apples. 'The Noble of the Woods,' he said quietly to himself, forging a smile. He breathed deeply and instantly felt himself relax. Sitting beneath the apple tree, all those years ago, had helped that little boy through hard times. The tree brought healing to his heart and strengthened his spirit. *Life can be difficult*, the tree would whisper in the wind. *You will always find your way.*

Deciding to take a break from writing, Peter collected his coat from the hall and stepped out of the house. It felt pleasantly warm beneath the gable and he stood for a few moments, listening to a wood-warbler fluting high in the cedar.

Making his way round the back of the house, he followed the path to the white arbour gate that led into Grandmother's garden. The archway was a mass of creamy blooms, each having a lemon heart, washed with cerise and highly scented. Of all the flowers growing in the garden, the Peace rose reminded him the most of his grandmother. Her unfailing love, her enduring spirit and hardiness to overcome any troubles. He stepped into the garden where the apple tree mantled the wall, and the combined fragrances of fruit and flower brought a fresh joy to his senses. Picking an apple and taking a large bite, Peter continued on his walk among pink heads of stonecrop, cheerful faces of asters and clusters of autumn crocuses.

Reaching the end of the path, he leaned against the wicker fence where grassy fields stretched out before him. A sudden wind came whipping, sending green blades falling and rising, like the waves of a sea. The breeze drew near and delicately washed his face.

Finishing his apple, core, pips and all, Peter wandered back through the garden and thought to check on Mr Toad parked under the carport. Removing a stray maple leaf caught on the windscreen wiper, he inspected the damage done to the headlamp: the glass lens was missing, and the chrome casing scuffed and dented.

'You're okay, Mr Toad,' he said, patting the bonnet. 'We'll get you fixed up. Everything will be good as new.'

Round the rear of the carport he straightened out two metal dustbins that were lost in the bushes and there on the ground noticed a small animal bone, clean of flesh. He rolled the bone with the toe cap of his boot. It was part of a rabbit's hind leg. With the tips of his fingers he picked up the bone and, lifting off a bin lid to toss it, unwittingly released a bevy of flies that swarmed out at him. Dropping the bone, slamming the lid, and with hands madly threshing, he swatted the flies from his face. Peter stood glaring at the dustbin, knowing that something awful was rotting there inside, and then noticed another swarm buzzing around the broad hibiscus.

On hands and knees, he went scrambling in the shallow ditch beneath the bush and there, in the under part, found another bone, festering, with fur and flesh still attached. The bone lay at the back of a small mound of earth and, with keen eye, Peter detected the faintest glint of metal hidden among the leaves. In prone position, he pulled himself deeper under the bush to get a closer look. Breaking off a low branch, he cautiously brushed the pile of leaves apart, revealing a small round metal plate, about three inches in diameter. Using the stick, he poked at the disc causing steel jaws to rear up out of the earth, gnashing its two rows of serrated teeth into the wood. Peter recoiled, recalling again the image of brown fur and blood-soaked paws.

'Morion?' he questioned aloud.

Four clamouring crows whirred low overhead. *Caaw, caaw, caaw, caaw* ...

Peter yanked the anchor chain from the earth and pulled the trap out onto the driveway. Staring at the monstrous contraption, he held a look of shock and horror, and his heart was thumping like a fist trying to get out of his chest. 'They say an old poacher makes the best gamekeeper!' His eyes went wandering the field. He looked up to the north ridge where the crows were circling, battling against a strong wind that made the forest roar.

The sun dipped behind the western hills and the air quickly chilled.

Peter hung the trap under the carport and wrapped the bone in old newspaper. Returning to the house, he left the bundle on the step by the door, deciding he would bury it in the morning. He glanced warily about the yard before going inside.

Against the cerulean canvas of twilight, the distant

sycamores appeared like inky-black drawings. The fields had all but surrendered to the night, becoming one singular nebulous form.

Turning from the window, Peter took up his reading glasses from where they rested on the carriage of the typewriter. Switching on the desk lamp he sat and focused on the type guide—the tiny space where type hammers strike the paper. While his hands hovered over the keytop, the image of the trap troubled his mind, and for some time he sat motionless, staring at the paper, waiting patiently for inspiration. His mind was not open and clear but kept playing out the vision of rotting bones, of those swarming, rapacious flies, the gruesome jaws of the trap, the steel teeth tearing through the earth. The dead otter.

Peter turned off the lamp, picked up the pheasant quill to fiddle with and rested back in the chair.

'Journey where your imagination runs wild and follow your heart,' were the departing words from his dear friend Brigit Dannan. Turning the feather between his fingers he recalled watching Brigit waving from the street corner the day he drove away from the apartment. He was missing her already; her enduring smile and catching laugh. Her cheerful heart had long been his comfort and refuge. She was a good friend, a loyal companion, much needed in a bustling city where one may easily feel lost and alone among the crowds. Remembering her standing on the pavement waving him goodbye brought a tear brimming. 'Journey where your imagination runs wild—' The telephone rang, startling Peter from his musing. He hurried to the kitchen and picked up the receiver.

'Hello.'

'Hello, Peter,' came a warm familiar voice.

'Brigit! Wow! I was just thinking of you, right this minute.' Peter wiped his eye.

'How's life down in Bumpkin Land?' asked Brigit.

'Everything's good here,' he answered. 'I've already revisited some of my old haunts and it's all just as I remembered. I feel I'm home again.'

'And how goes the writing, Mr P.J. Goodhope?' He heard her chuckle.

'I'm already getting a few ideas down, just as they come. The valley, the woods and fields are a true inspiration.'

'Have you heard from Rooks Removals?' Brigit

asked. 'They rang me to say they've found a painting of yours left in their lorry. It was tucked up behind some blankets. Going by the description of "birds over marshlands", it sounds like *The Migration*.'

Peter eyed the stack of canvases on the kitchen table and the many boxes lining the hallway.

'I hadn't noticed. I haven't even started unpacking, just a few important things like pens and paints. Maybe come for a visit soon and bring the drawing down with you. Get Rooks to deliver it over to you first. How did the audition go?'

'It went really well; I got the part! We go into pre-production next week. I'm playing the role of Clover the carthorse. Should be a lot of fun. The prosthetics are superb, the makeup is *amazing*.' Her voice skirled. 'The animal masks look so realistic, like they become part of your face!'

'That's great news. Congratulations, Clover!'

'Yeee-aaaay,' he heard Brigit guffawing over the sound of a distant car horn. 'Must dash, Poppy's pulled up outside in a taxi; we're going out for a celebration dinner. I'll call you in a few days. We can talk about me coming for a visit then. Oh, by the way, Poppy got the part of Muriel the goat!'

'Well, say hello to Muriel for me, and order an extra bowl of carrots on the side,' Peter laughed. 'So good to hear your voice. I miss you, Brigit.' There came a moment of silence. 'Thanks for calling. Enjoy yourselves tonight.'

'We will,' Brigit replied. 'Keep writing.'

'I will.'

The conversation went quiet again.

'Is everything all right with you?' Brigit asked.

'All good.'

'Okay, bye for now then.'

'Bye, Brigit.'

He heard the sound of static, of her hanging up the phone. Goodbyes never came easy. Even then he waited a moment more, hoping she might still be there. Comforted from having heard her voice, he smiled and returned the receiver to its hook.

Turning on the desk lamp, Peter placed a portable scribal desk next to the typewriter and positioned a piece of paper on it. Picking up the bottle of ink he'd found in the drawer, he began studying the homemade label, reminiscing on how Grandmother used to make her own ink from oak galls.

'Oak galls grow after a special kind of wasp has

laid her eggs on the underside of an oak leaf,' said his grandmother. 'As the larva develops, the tree responds by releasing tannic and gallic acid that forms a small shell around the growing pupa, about the size of a marble.' Young boy Peter rolled the spongy nut in the palm of his hand. 'Some folk call it an oak apple,' said Grandmother. 'It acts both as a protection for the tree, and home for the wasp.' She took a dozen dry galls and began crushing them with mortar and pestle. 'Make sure you see a tiny hole in the shell; it indicates the wasp has matured and vacated its home.' She soaked the pulverised galls in a pint of rainwater, adding a secret ingredient: a glass of her homemade blackberry wine. 'It's all about the gradual fermentation,' she would say, 'for the oak apples to release their precious acids.' It would take two weeks before the final stage: the straining of the liquid through cheesecloth. 'This is where the magic begins!' He watched as Grandmother sprinkled a spoonful of green vitriol to the brown solution, instantly turning it black. 'Don't forget a little acacia gum,' she piped. 'It's the resin from the acacia tree and it adds brilliancy and body!' Young Peter looked on with wonderment as his grandmother held a small piece of golden-coloured sap up to the light. The crystals were dropped and dissolved into the final mix before the ink was bottled, corked, and sealed with wax.

Removing the wax with his penknife, Peter uncorked the bottle and filled the inkwell of the scribal desk. Adjusting the writing angle to 45 degrees, he dipped his quill pen and began making bold, sweeping marks across the virgin sheet. Running smooth as silk, the ink at first appeared grey on paper, then, over a few seconds, darkened as it oxidised to a rich purplish-black. He made several vertical lines, then horizontal and oblique. Peter was most at ease when drawing, and any cares or troubles of the day would instantly flee his mind. Lost in a world of ink, he scratched and scribbled, producing tiny crosshatches, adding further vertical lines, more horizontal, as he sketched out the brace and pickets of a wooden gate. Dipping the pen again, he next made short and long curling strokes, thick and thin, super fine hairlines—each depending on the amount of pressure he applied to the nib—developing light and shade in the drawing. Finishing with random squiggles of repeating patterns, he rendered the gatepost, with its hanging chain, locking latch and glimpses of the field beyond.

After adding just a few short stems of cowslip among the scribble-hatch grass, he popped in a few unfurled poppies, their heads bowing to the ground. By the foot of the post, he rendered a single finger-stall, a foxglove bell in bloom, and in all of thirty minutes he had sketched the entire scene. Stippling the last few conical shapes of wood knots into the gate and applying striation strokes to create the wood cleaves, Peter was finally done. The picture seemed almost perfect, yet something was amiss; something strangely wanting. Musing, reclining back in his chair, he quite imagined a little owl fly up from the field and land on the gatepost. For the shortest moment the owl looked at Peter, blinking its bright yellow eyes.

The moon silvered the sycamores and bathed Hope House in the palest blue light.

Anam flew up onto the gatepost and sat watchful, turning his gaze towards the house while above the rooftop circled Otus, cautiously surveying the ground below.

Hoo, hoo-oo—'How did I ever manage to get caught up in all this nonsense?' Otus grumbled to himself, landing on the roof gable and folding his wings. From his high vantage point, he looked drearily about him and noticed Lúnasa Mouse making a dash across the ground below. Watching the small rodent scurrying triggered his appetite, but it was neither time nor place to be thinking of filling his stomach. The mouse disappeared beneath the hibiscus bush. Otus swung his head almost a full turn to peer down at Anam sitting on the post. Anam was watching the human figure passing across the glowing window.

Hoo, hoo-oo, Otus called soberly.

Woo-hik, answered Anam with a brightly chirp.

They waited.

Peter was hard-working the Imperial, striking its keys with the greatest of ease.

Pushing back the carriage, he yawned and stretched his aching arms, ready to retire for the night. The sheet of paper was pulled from the platen and placed on a mounting pile of typed pages.

A few embers glowed in the fireplace. He threw on a large ash log, hoping it would burn slowly through the night.

Moving down the hallway turning out the lights, Peter was still troubled by his finding of the trap and hesitated when he was about to lock the house. Instead of turning the key, he lifted the latch and opened the door a few inches, half-expecting someone on the other side. Switching on the porch light, he looked down at the wrapped bone lying on the doorstep. 'Perhaps,' said Peter to himself, 'whoever set the trap will come back.' Stepping onto the driveway, he felt a whip of cold air and heard the maples stir.

From the gatepost, Anam looked eagerly at the newcomer. Otus kept a watchful look from the rooftop, turning his head as Peter crossed the gravel and disappeared into the shadow of the carport. Spreading his wings, Otus glided silently to the ground. He turned to Anam, who began jigging on the post, bouncing up and down, eyes wide, encouraging his comrade to move closer towards the house, to the threshold of the human world.

Otus waddled along on his short stumpy legs, stopping at the bundle of newspaper. His mind grew curious, and he began to tear at it with beak and claw. The rabbit foot slipped off the step and rolled out at his feet. With a shrill and flap of wings, Otus jumped backwards. Looking over at Anam, he saw the human returning across the way carrying a bonebreaker, heard its chain rattling along the ground. A piercing shriek and a sideways hop sent Otus springing into the air, wings whipping into a powerful lift. *Whek-WHEK-whek.* 'Stealer-STEALER-Stealer!' Otus gave the warning. Peter glimpsed the owl just before it vanished around the side of the house. Immediately behind him came another cry, a high keening, as Anam leapt from the gatepost, *Ke-ik!* Peter watched as the bird flew straight past him, flitting up over the roof.

Anam looked down at the newcomer standing by the steps, the bonebreaker dangling from his hands. In the field beyond the gatepost, he spotted a shadowy shape moving in the grass—it was Sion Fox, wending his way towards Hope House. Hearing the commotion of the clamouring owls, Sion stopped short and sniffed the air.

'Otus, wait.' Anam flapped his wings wildly. 'Otus!' he cried out. 'How was I to know?' Anam pursued Otus, who had already reached the sycamores.

'You fool, Anam!' Otus began screeching like a cat. 'You nearly got us both killed! He was carrying a bonebreaker! Now drop this nonsense and leave me alone. GET OUT OF MY SIGHT!' Otus banked sharply, heading home to Tinne Nook. Anam stopped the chase, watched as Otus dived down into the long shadows and disappeared between field and sky.

'This has to be a mistake,' Anam cried anxiously, passing swiftly along the line of sycamores. 'I was sure it was Fireun.'

Anam came to rest on the tie beam of Beith Barn. He smoothed his feathers and gathered his thoughts.

'This human is the one. I know it, I feel it in my blood. But why did he carry the bonebreaker? Was he making ready to trap Sion Fox?'

In his heart, he knew the human was not a stealer, but doubt troubled his mind.

'There's only one way to find out.' And from the barn he flew, back into the night.

Diaphanous cloud covered the sky, producing a prismatic halo around the moon. Hope House stood bathed in a magical glow.

In a sidelong sweep Anam alighted on the post.

All was quiet. Not a light shone from any window. He sat, waiting, watching for signs of movement. He so desperately wanted this human to be the one. Seeing him down by Saille Lake, there had been something about his presence that was pleasing. He'd felt no threat from him, nor sensed any danger— as if the human belonged there with the trees, with the water and the mist. And inside Beith Barn ... had he sensed a shared camaraderie?

From the silence came a sudden noise. Anam moved his head rhythmically in a circular motion, eyes fixed upon the house. He heard a rustling, low murmurings and heavy breathing, but not from the direction he was looking. With facial discs turned to the field, Anam could tune at different distances, hearing even the faintest crackle of grass trodden underfoot.

He observed a strange glow, a small orb of light, moving along the field. The light changed direction and was now coming straight towards him. Anam felt his heart pounding as if outside his chest.

The ball of light was drawing nearer. The sound of heavy breathing getting closer. 'What am I thinking? I'm an owl, I should fly!' Instinct was to leave but intuition kept his head locked, eyes fixed and talons firm to the post.

Humans were fast approaching, three of them, cutting through the long grass.

'Stealers!' Anam yelped uncontrollably. It was too late to fly now—they were sure to see him. Certain to be carrying a thunderfire!

Jonas pointed the torchlight towards the fence as Fenning handed Morgan the gun and climbed over. They did not notice the little owl, rigid as the post he sat on. The three men crept like cats along the driveway. Anam knew them. He recalled one dark awful night when the stealers stole poor Connie's family; a whole warren of rabbits dug straight from the earth. Poor Connie—she never stood a chance. All her little kits snatched away as they lay sleeping.

What would stealers be doing visiting the newcomer? Anam wondered. He watched as two of the men slipped beneath the hibiscus bush, while the other stood guard, clutching the thunderfire.

Anam flew from the gatepost up to the roof gable. He could hear the two stealers down below, growling under the bush.

'Damn you, Fenning! Where did you set the

trap?'

'Right here! I set it right here!'

'Keep your voices down,' hissed Morgan, peering through the bush, 'you'll wake the enemy. What's taking you so long?'

'Shut it!' came a barking reply.

Anam wanted a closer look. He fluttered soundlessly to the ground next to Morgan's feet and scurried under the bush. There were the two stealers, one clutching the other's throat.

'You blundering fool, you damn fiddlehead,' said Jonas. 'Don't you see what this means? Brain-drain for us all!'

Fenning gasped for air. Jonas kept his thumbs pressed into his windpipe.

'I believe this belongs to you?' came a solemn voice.

The two men looked up. Anam spun around. Peter was on the driveway holding the trap. He poked a torch through the branches, illuminating the startled faces of the two men.

'And I believe this belongs to you,' came a voice from behind.

Before he could turn, Peter felt a staggering

blow to the back of his head. The trap slipped from his hand, his world went black, and he fell face-down into the bush.

Anam let out a repeating *Kee-ik-kee-ik!* Then, scurrying from the foliage, wings madly flapping, he took off for the safety of the sky.

Cocksure, Morgan stood clutching the barrel end of the rifle.

'Quick everyone, let's get out of here!' rasped Jonas, hurrying out from under the bush. 'Good work, Morgan; grab the trap and let's go.'

Watching on the wing, Anam could see the steal-ers scampering up the lane, heard the padding of their feet upon the road and when they were lost to sight, and the echo of that clinking chain died away, he came back down and landed on the roof.

A warm muzzle pushed against Peter's cheek. Then a long wet tongue began licking him on the back of the head. Nudging his shoulder gently, Sion stirred Peter back to wakefulness. Peter rolled over. With eyes half open, he gazed up at the fox standing over him.

'You are the one,' came a low gruff, but Peter could not see who had spoken the words. Dazed and glassy-eyed, he looked vacantly upon the fox.

'Help us, Fireun,' said the voice again. 'Save us from the stealers.'

Confluence

rigit handed the wrapped painting over to the guard, who placed it inside a luggage van while she boarded the train. She would arrive in Nemeton just before noon.

She paced along the corridor in search of a quiet carriage, her chestnut-red hair jouncing over her shoulders. With beaming smiles, she greeted her fellow commuters.

After a long week of rehearsals, Brigit was needing to escape for the weekend. Late nights, early starts, meant skipping meals and missing sleep. She longed for a good night's rest, some home-style cooking, and maybe a brisk walk in the country air would help revive her. Besides, she wanted to surprise Peter and make sure he was settling in to his new-found life.

She checked her watch: 7.29. The train guard blew his whistle. Brigit found a compartment where an elderly man was struggling to put a briefcase onto the luggage rack. She gave the man a helping hand just as the train jolted from the station, shunting Brigit gracelessly across the carriage floor. She laughed at her own embarrassment and, easing the knapsack from her back, took a seat by the window. A young girl sat opposite; her hair braided with strands of coloured silk. She glanced up from reading her book.

'Travelling far?' Brigit asked the girl.

'All the way to the coast,' the girl replied, smiling.

'Nice.'

'And you?' said the girl.

'I'm on my way to Nemeton to see a friend.' Brigit brushed a curl from her cheek.

'Nemeton? The town that time forgot.'

Brigit looked at the girl, wondering what she meant.

The girl smiled assuredly. 'It's a charming village,'

she laughed, 'like a little piece of paradise.' The girl went back to reading her book. Brigit studied the triskelion image on the book's cover, a symbol of three conjoined spirals, then turned and gazed pensively out of the window, watching all the workings of a busy city slip silently by.

At the head of the bench sat Balorid, Dearg on his right. The flickering light of the lantern played about their grim faces. Sitting opposite, Jonas, Morgan and Fenning appeared guilty as charged. The trap lay on the table.

'Morgan knocked him out cold, good and proper he did,' said Jonas. 'He won't remember a thing. We took the trap and got the hell away.'

'Like we were never there,' added Fenning, nodding to his colleagues, urging for moral support. In turn, they looked at one another, shrugged their shoulders in mutual agreement. 'Like we were never there,' they chorused, adding nothing more to their defence.

Balorid sat in long silence, casting a stone-cold stare at the three miscreants. His chair grated on the floor as he slowly rose from the table and then began to pace the floor. Morgan, Fenning and Jonas could only but look at Balorid's wrinkled eyelid, fearing signs of it opening.

'So you went to Hope House to check on a trap but ended up getting caught yourselves?'

Shamed, the men hung their heads. Amused, Dearg let out a low snigger and lit a cigarette.

The one-eyed monster approached the three men, reeling off the details of their misdemeanours: 'So far, Goodhope has witnessed a dead otter, a buzzard and a box of crows in a gamekeeper's van, discovered one of our traps on his land, poked a flashlight into two of your pug-ugly faces and been struck on the head by the butt of a gun.' Balorid grimaced while considering the details. 'You say it's like you were never there!?' The men exchanged pitiful glances with one another. They each saw Balorid's beastly eyelid twitching. 'You really believe Goodhope is thinking he imagined all this? Dreamt it up?' Balorid leaned in towards the men, fist poised and ready to strike. Dearg flicked out his tongue with renewed amusement.

'What to do, what to do,' pondered Balorid. Then, lowering his hand, he began drumming his bony fingers on the table. He leaned across and pulled Morgan's hat firmly over his frizzy hair, teasing him as it were. 'Not a pretty picture,' he stated to the foolish witling.

Poker-faced, the three lackeys waited anxiously for the verdict.

'BAH!' Like the striking of a gavel, Balorid smashed his fist hard down on the table, his evil eye half-peering out from its sunken socket. Breaths were held—lives hung in the balance. The eyelid closed again. 'We let this whole thing blow over,' Balorid decided, bringing instant relief to the accused. 'Goodhope is a tiny thorn in the backside of big business.' With his one seeing eye, he glared at the men. 'If any of this leaks, if word gets out we are trapping wild animals for profit, our entire operation could be ruined. One more mistake, however trivial, and it's brain-drain for the lot of you.' Balorid raised his fist, ready again to smite the table. 'Do I make myself clear!?'

Jonas, Fenning and Morgan nodded gleefully, relieved by their acquittal.

Balorid paced the floor. 'We have international connections, business is growing, sales increasing.

I need deer, foxes and rabbits—I want weasels, squirrels, hawks and badgers.' Balorid stood back at the head of the table, scowling. 'Owls have been spotted by Tinne Nook. Forget the nets, forget the snares, just take the guns to them!' Turning to Dearg, his scowling changed to a look of mild admiration. 'Dearg has the masterful hands of a true taxidermist when it comes to concealing deadly wounds.' Dearg returned a nod and a wink, grateful for the passing compliment.

'Stay off Hope Land, find other places to trap,' Balorid ordered. 'A large consignment is on the horizon. We've just received another order for a fox and falcon mount, so prepare two more crates ready for the evening train. I'll deliver them to the station myself this afternoon.' Balorid rested his hand on Dearg's shoulder. 'Maestro—if you please, it's time to unveil your latest masterpiece.' Dearg scurried off his chair, disappeared through to the kitchen where dim lights of candles flickered on the ceiling. Facing the men, Balorid stretched out his arms in a palm-down display. The room went silent.

Dearg reappeared, wheeling a metal trolley bearing his most recent works. A mounted roe deer stood on artificial grass staring fixedly, its limbs out-stretched, and head held high as if sniffing the air. Beside the baby creature crouched a fox cast in the act of snarling. Mocking the scene, Dearg stooped to the level of the stuffed fox, showing off his own set of gruesome teeth. Such slapstick brought a roar of laughter, followed by applause. Revealing his next piece, Dearg held up a glass dome housing a falcon perched on a gnarled bough, its hooked beak tearing out the entrails of a field mouse.

Balorid clapped his hands wildly as Dearg gave a theatrical bow.

'Dearg, you're a genius,' praised Balorid. 'You make the critters look more alive than they did in real life!' He turned to his lickspittles, throwing them another cold, empty stare. 'From here on there'll be no more screw-ups,' he gritted. 'We are world leaders in the science of taxidermy, we provide a special ser-vice to the elite, and it is them we ultimately serve.'

From Dearg's trolley, Balorid began sorting through a collection of surgical instruments: spring scissors, a pair of forceps, brain scoop, a bone cutter, finally taking up a scalpel which he proceeded to stab at a large map of Nemeton pinned on the wall.

'We work these places for now—here and here.' The scalpel left stab marks in the areas of Ferne Stone and Tinne Nook. 'And here!' Balorid plunged the scalpel into the region of Ghostwood, leaving the blade embedded in the map. Turning, he leaned across the table. 'Keep away from Hope House ... until we find a way to rid ourselves of Goodhope.'

Brigit stepped off the train just before noon. Deciding it was easier to leave the painting at the station where she and Peter could collect it later in the car, she handed it over to the stationmaster, who placed the picture on a rack with other items awaiting collection.

Out on the forecourt, Brigit was greeted by a solitary taxi driver hopeful for a fare. She smiled and gestured her preference to walk. The cabby kindly doffed his hat and returned to reading his newspaper.

Preparing to dash across the road in her usual fashion, Brigit found neither traffic nor pedestrian to negotiate, only a girl with long flaxen hair trotting by on a handsome white horse. It was as if she had stepped into another age, another world. She stood a moment just to enjoy the peace and tranquillity. It was easy to understand Peter's want for change to leave the city. The air was clean and soothing to the soul, the light soft and hazy, pleasing on the eye. How quiet and serene, how sweetly the birds sang. Nemeton did indeed appear like a little piece of paradise.

Awen River babbled beneath a packhorse bridge. Leaning on the low parapet under the shade of an elm, Brigit breathed deeply, stilling her mind. Gazing down upon the quiet water, quite unexpectedly, she glimpsed a water vole, his low profile pushing a ream on the surface as he crossed from one bank to the other before disappearing into a bed of reeds. Then came a small white duck, sculling upstream, dipping its bright yellow bill into the long river grass.

'Oh, hello, Jemima. Nice day for a paddle!' said Brigit with a chuckle.

Carina Duck looked sideways up at her then started quacking in a most disgruntled fashion, as if to rebuke Brigit for mistaking her identity. The duck turned about and paddled back downstream. Brigit's jaw dropped, her mouth agape, laughing at the bird's gruff remark and rather rude exit!

Continuing over the bridge, feeling the sun warming on her shoulders, Brigit suddenly looked up to the sound of a shocking noise—like a gunshot. Looming towards her came a van trailing a cloud of blue smoke. Pushing against the parapet, she lifted her scarf up around her mouth as the Bedford rattled by. She glanced backwards at the spoilt scene, at that dreadful van.

Stepping off the bridge, the road divided two ways. A signpost read *Nemeton Green* one way, *Town Centre* the other. On the street corner stood a greengrocer's shop and Brigit paused at the colourful display of vegetables sitting inside rows of wooden crates. She took a shopping basket and picked out the yellowest sweetcorn, the fattest parsnip, gathered up a bunch of carrots, a leek and small cauliflower then stepped inside the shop. The man behind the counter looked up with a warming smile.

'A very good morning,' the grocer said, pushing his cloth cap above his brow, revealing a twinkle in his eye.

'Good morning.' Brigit beamed. 'Soup is on the menu.'

'A fine meal that be on any day of the week, miss,' he answered cheerily.

From her basket, Brigit placed her goods on the counter and with wide enquiring eyes, looked at the shopkeeper. 'Could you please tell me the way to Hope House? I'm on foot and I don't have a map.'

The shopkeeper began to weigh the carrots. 'Let's see now ... Hope House ... ah, that be right at the bottom of Muin Lane, miss. Take the road through the village, past the pond, and follow it all the way up to the rise.' Weighing the cauliflower, he continued, 'Keep going about a mile, and you'll come back down the rise. Hope House lies at the bottom of the lane, you'll see the sign and white gates.' The man paused, raised an eyebrow, and pulled forward his cap, holding a parsnip in midair. 'Mind you keep to the lane by the stone wall, miss, where the road dips down,' he said gravely. 'Don't go wandering off onto the north ridge and getting lost in Ghostwood. Kind folk have been known to go missing up in those woods.' While the parsnip and corn were being weighed Brigit puzzled at the shopkeeper. There was an odd air about him all of a sudden, a strange foreboding about his warning her of the woods. *Local folklore, no doubt.* She shrugged it off and hastened to pack the vegetables into her knapsack.

'Thank you, kind sir.' Brigit bid farewell, and went on her way.

Passing the quaint cottages around the village pond, she followed the winding road leading up to the rise. There along the upper lane, bramble hedges were bursting with blackberries. She could not help but stop to taste them, each one plump, juicy and sweet and so irresistibly moreish! Within a short time, a dozen berries slipped passed her lips.

Walking under the dappled light beneath a row of dainty birch, Brigit was soon accompanied by Dreean Wren. How delightful to watch the tiniest of birds, its round brown body flitting ahead of her, filling the hedges with such clear, shrill notes. Brigit felt a sense of inner renewal and increased liveliness and onwards, over the rise she skipped, leaving the village behind.

The church chimed the hour as Brigit passed the wooden lychgate. Older than the churchyard in which it stood, a centuries-old yew cast a long shadow across the path. Concealed within the tree's evergreen branches perched Gavina Hawk, eyes watching, unflinching, as Brigit strolled by.

In a short time, Brigit reached the drystone wall and stood staring out along the winding tracks of the ridge leading to Ghostwood. *Mind you keep to the lane by the stone wall—Don't go wandering off and getting lost.* Heeding the shopkeeper's warning, she began her descent down the lane.

Brigit came at last to a driveway, and on her right a small wooden sign read: *Hope House.* She walked gaily up the gravelled drive, through the open gates and along the row of glowing maples.

Peter's car was parked facing out from under the carport. 'Good afternoon, Mr Toad,' she called in jest, then with a puzzled look she noticed the broken headlamp.

Brigit stepped up to the oak door and delicately touched the intricate wood carving. Lifting the brass fox brush, she knocked three times before trying the latch.

'Hello? Anyone home?' She opened the door. 'Peter, are you there? It's me, Brigit.' She walked along the hallway strewn with packing boxes and, putting her knapsack on the kitchen table, wandered into the living room. With a quick glance at Peter's desk, she approached the bay window. Drinking in the stunning views of fields and glades, her eye was drawn towards the distant sycamores standing in a straight line against the sky. Then northward she gazed, at the sombre pines of Ghostwood that shadowed the north ridge. A solitary crow cawed as it passed the window.

On the desk, next to the antique typewriter, lay Peter's pens and pencils, ink pots and paper. On the scribal desk hung a sketching of an owl perched on a gatepost. Brigit smiled at the whimsical drawing and as she turned, there stood Peter, his face drawn and pale. She gave a sudden gasp, raising her hands to her mouth.

'Good heavens, Peter! What's happened?'

Over a pot of tea, Peter told Brigit all about the poachers. He sounded vague, indefinite as to what time or day it happened.

'I must have blanked out for a few seconds but when I came round ... I saw this fox ... standing right over me. And it spoke to me.' Peter looked at Brigit, but it was though he stared right through her. '*You are the one*, the voice said. *Save us from the stealers.*'

Realising the seriousness of the matter, Brigit

placed her teacup on the table and reached for Peter's hand.

'We should get you checked out. You might have concussion.'

Even in that moment of gravity Brigit's face was calm, her voice soothing and Peter smiled warmly at her. With a widening grin, he leaned across the table, taking her by both hands. 'It's not just a kiss that awakes true love from the spell of sleep; your smile alone would easily break the charm.' She warmed and caressed his hands. 'In your eyes I see happy ever after,' Peter added.

A shyness came over Brigit, though quickly veiled. Withdrawing her hands, she sipped her tea. 'This is serious, Peter,' she said with a shade of sobriety, peering at him over her cup. 'What a dreadful thing to happen.'

'I'm fine, Brigit, it's just a bump. I've had worse.' Peter sat back, looking more relaxed and cheerful. The third cup of tea had helped bring light and colour back to his face. 'Makes for a good story though, don't you think?' he said, holding a mischievous grin.

At Saille Lake, Anam was sitting in the hanging branches of the willow, watching a million mayflies dancing about the surface of the lake. In the water below he saw his own troubled reflection and gave a doleful cry. Otus would have nothing more to do with him; he had cast him out. Anam let out several long piercing shrills at the thought of losing a father, a friend, a mentor. Now he was all alone in the world. His pitiful calls made the lake seem a more lonesome place.

The idea of revisiting Dru kept entering his mind, but he pushed the notion away and looked down again upon the dimpling water, the surface now bronzed with hungry carp feeding on flies hatching by their hundreds in the afternoon sun.

There was an undying urge to do something—but what? He recalled Dru's parting words: 'There will be many dangers to face and difficulties to overcome. Go do what you must do. Return here in three days.'

'Must I really go back to see Dru?' Anam mewed sorrowfully. 'What will he think of me?' A monster carp left the water, gulping a mouthful of flies, leaving a tidal ring in its wake. 'It's too dangerous to fly over Ghostwood. No bird would dare do so alone, not by choice, not knowing of the terrible tales.' He looked across at the beech tree on the opposite shore, at the gregarious birds flitting among its highest branches. 'Only foolish rooks and crows would be careless enough to cross the forbidden forest.'

Anam dug his talons deep into the pendulous wand, his young heart yearning to find an answer. Again, he stifled the persistent voice rising deep inside, urging him to return to the ancient oak. In a bid to escape his inner turmoil, Anam took to the air.

He came fast over the water, rising and falling, passing up along the stream that coursed into the lake, then above the knoll he flew, cutting through the birch wood. Unstopping, he swept clear over Beith Barn and came out along the row of sycamores. Heading straight towards the north ridge, he kept shy of Ghostwood, and with brisk wingbeats tracked above the scalloped wall, occasionally throwing a glance up at the ghostly trees that towered above.

A half mile and the boundary wall curved north-west where he left the belt of dark woods behind.

Wizened hazel trees grew in a circle around Coll Spring; a sacred place of confluence, where three subterranean streams flowed up through the ground, spilling down the rocky hillside. Adjacent to the well, a spinney of ash, aspen and hawthorn grew. Shielded under the shade of a flourishing alder tree, four standing stones stood in a square formation; a block of dolomite rested across the columns which formed a natural shelter. Anam had found his way to Ferne Stone. It was here Sion Fox lived. It was his home.

It was uncustomary for one species of bird to talk to another, let alone a bird commune with a fox, but times were changing. Anam knew the day drew near when animals would unite in a final bid to reconcile their differences and find a new way to coexist and safeguard their future.

Anam assessed the detritus ground, where heather, furze and thistle thrived among the ancient boulders. And there was Sion, sprawled out under the great stone table.

Anam perched in a curling branch, at once camouflaged among the hazelnuts.

Sion pretended not to notice the owl. He knew

of Anam—had seen him many times flying over Hope Land and, more recently, lingering around Hope House. He knew the owl had been there on the night of the stealers.

Anam sat contemplating his next move, unsure of his approach.

'How does an owl even begin to speak to a fox?' he hooted softly.

'The same way a fox speaks to an owl,' came an instant reply.

Startled, Anam peered down at Sion, who still appeared to be sleeping.

Cocking his eye, Sion looked up. 'I know you're there, Anam,' he said with a low gruff. 'I feel the same way as you. We animals must band together.'

Anam was taken back, about to take an airborne leap when Sion opened his other eye and sat upright. 'We need to talk, Little Owl, about the new-comer. I too have looked into his eyes. I saw no sign of vulgar beast, but affinity with our own kind.'

Anam swivelled his head, one way then the other, in search of another bird out to make a fool of him. But he was surely alone.

'You looked into the eye of the newcomer,

Sion?' asked Anam, testing out the possibility of being able to talk with a fox.

'The human never meant you or Otus any harm. In fact, he saved me from the bonebreaker that night.' Sion's ears pricked. 'But we never made contact. Before the human could receive the spirit of anima, he lost consciousness.'

Anam lifted a talon to scratch his head; he ruffled his feathers and frowned at Sion. He puzzled on how they could be talking in the same language! Being raised by a long-eared owl, he knew that one family can commune with another. But owl and fox? Was it perhaps a psychic connection? He remembered as a fledgling in the nest, how he had always known when Otus was returning home. Anam even felt Dru had recently been trying to persuade him back to his hollow by thought alone—but never had he known one animal species to be able to commune with another.

'I believe the newcomer is Fireun, the one Dru foretold,' said Anam, now casting away any shred of doubt. Throwing chance to the wind he flew down to Sion, who, having sauntered out from under the refuge of the rock, sat casually grooming his paw.

'Don't fret, Little Owl—all that is happening is meant to be.'

Anam and Sion began speaking in earth's ancient language, once understood by all living things. They spent the afternoon forming a close friendship, knowing in some strange and mysterious way they had always shared an alliance, a common connection.

Anam learned how Sion was orphaned as a cub, when barely old enough to fend or forage for himself. His mother had died in a bonebreaker and by the thunderfire his father was taken. For three long and lonely days, young Sion did not dare venture from the den. He grew up alone, relying purely on his instincts. He told Anam how being secluded at such a tender age had forced him to become a recluse among the rocks. 'A hermit of the hills,' he quipped.

Anam spoke of Dru and his prophetic vision of a human that, by animal initiation, would become their saviour, helping them to eradicate the stealers and so put an end to the senseless cruelty and the slaughtering of innocent lives.

'Our future depends on Fireun,' said Anam. 'Only he can help us unite and bring about a peaceful

change, show us how we can all live in harmony.'
Anam expressed how he already felt changed—how
he seemed to think differently, act differently, knowing there was more to life than just being an owl of
the woods.

Sion shared his views on the devious, cunning
ways of humans, yet not once did he ever express
bitterness or contempt towards the species, only
teaching Anam to look upon mankind with caution
and suspicion.

In the changing light, as the evening drew near,
they shared their views on the future of their habitat, amicably agreeing on the growing urgency to
gather up all the animals of wood and field to teach
them about the inevitable changes that were
coming.

The sun dipped behind the hills, tinting the
slopes red and bringing a cool change. Already the
brightest star was on the rise and twinkling back.

Fox and owl talked late into the night, planning
and puzzling over how they might replace fear with
hope. It was agreed Sion would attempt another
encounter with the newcomer. They had to know
whether the human was able to receive the spirit of

anima and, if so, prove he was indeed Fireun.

The moon had risen above the trees when Anam bid farewell to Sion. He started back to Beith Barn, his heart brimming with hopes and dreams, feeling exuberant at having found a kindred spirit. With wings swift and strong, carrying him higher than ever before, he soared across the moonlit sky. 'What friendship! What providence!' he hooted, knowing that he and Sion would help save their world.

The cold air washed over him while the land dipped farther away. How he wished this night would last forever. Faster and faster his wings beat and though he was but a little owl, his eyes were fierce with the fire that burned in him.

Then Anam heard a long, harsh scream—*Shee! Shee!*—'Anam, come down, you're flying too high. You're drifting too far!' It was Dru calling to him, far across the valley.

Dropping back to earth, Anam became unsure of his whereabouts. He'd lost track of his bearings, and all landmarks were gone. Beneath his wings, spreading mile after mile, was a dense dark forest. With sudden panic he shrieked, *Kiew-eek!* 'Ghost-wood!' The sound of his cry carried on the air.

Circling low over a small clearing of trees, Anam saw the flash of fire, heard the thunder. A cold fear gripped his heart. 'Thunderfire!' he cried out. The spent shot hummed past his face, a single pellet grazed his breast, nicked the skin and drew blood. Anam's wings buckled as he spiralled out of control. Another gunshot, and he plummeted from the sky, dropping like a stone to the ground.

A New Light

A squall threw open the bedroom window—curtains billowing. Instantly awake, Peter sat up in bed, causing Brigit to turn in her sleep. He heard a familiar voice, a cry on the wind.

You are the one, Fireun, said the squall. It came in short gusts, repeating the same words. *You are the one, Fireun.* Then the tempest suddenly calmed, the ghostly utterance faded, and the curtains came to rest upon the sill. Realising he'd been dreaming, Peter lay down, pressed his head into the pillow and in a few seconds was asleep again.

Anam's eyes twitched and opened. He could hear the

scuffling of stealers close by and then a light pierced the darkness.

'Morgan, over here,' came a hushed voice. 'I heard something.' Jonas searched about the forest floor with a hunter's spotlight.

'Most likely it dropped down over by that dead tree,' rasped Morgan. 'Shine the torch over here.'

Anam felt his heart beating through the ground as the light passed over him, his dappled plumage camouflaging him among the mouldering leaves.

'Come on, doubt we'll find it,' said Jonas. 'Good shot taking a bird out on the wing. Let's now try our luck up by the ridge—it's usually good for a few pheasants, maybe we'll bag ourselves a grouse or two.'

The stealers trudged off. Anam dared not move. He hunkered down and only when the forest was silent did he restfully close his eyes.

Peter opened his eyes.

He looked at Brigit sleeping by his side. Never before had he seen her look so serene, with the moonlight shining through the window, glowing upon the fine lineaments of her face. He studied the lock of hair tossed about her cheek; her soft mouth curled in a rested smile.

'Sweet dreams,' he whispered, and crept out of bed.

The wind was blustering again, whipping the curtains. Peter went over to close the window. The moon was now high on the eastern rise, radiant above the church where small water-cart clouds raced across the sky. About to fasten the window latch, his eye was drawn down to the garden. The fox stood under the apple tree looking up at him. The animal began to bark. Each monosyllabic yip and yap seemed to mimic human speech. By some strange power or spell, Peter could understand what the animal was saying. He heard the words loud and clear.

'I-am Si-on,' the fox barked.

Man and beast looked unwaveringly at one another, neither moving a muscle. The wind stopped blowing, the curtains hung at rest. Peter leaned out the window.

'What do you want from me?' he called down.

'Save-us-from-the-stea-lers,' barked Sion.

Peter's mind reeled. It would be madness to

believe he could understand what the fox was saying—lunacy to think he could commune with it!

'I must still be asleep,' he reasoned, closing the window. He sat down on the bed, folding his hands in his lap. *But this is not a dream.* Lying down, he pulled the bedcovers over himself.

'Save-us! Save-us! Save-us!' the fox kept barking from the garden.

The morning sun crowned the hills to the sound of pealing bells.

Peter lay listening to the last strident chime ring and fade. Noticing Brigit was already up, he threw back the covers, jumped out of bed and opened the window. The cold morning air washed his face, revitalised and sharpened his senses. The daylight seemed brighter than usual, colours more vivid, clear and striking. From distant sycamores came the clarion cry of a blue jay and more distant, the faint bleating of a lost lamb calling for its mother.

Looking down over the garden wall, there was no sign of the fox by the tree.

He could hear Brigit downstairs pattering about in the kitchen; the aroma of brewing coffee further stirred his senses. Peter tied his robe and left the room.

Brigit appeared at the foot of the stairs, wearing an orange hibiscus flower in her hair. 'Morning, Peter. Breakfast is served,' she smiled up. 'How are you feeling this morning?'

'Fan-tas-tic!' replied Peter. 'How about you? Sleep well?'

'Best night's rest I've had in ages. It's so quiet and peaceful here.'

He noticed the sun streaming along the hall and how it lit up her hair in an aurora of colours; scarlet, crimson and carmine. She turned and started back to the kitchen, singing to herself:

'All things bright and beautiful ...'

Standing on the balcony, acting the *primo uomo*, Peter broke out in modest tenor voice: 'All creatures, great and small,' then strode off to the bathroom.

Splashing his face with water, he looked in the mirror. 'The friend of nature is the man who feels himself inwardly united with everything that lives in nature, who shares in the fate of all creatures, helps them when he can in their pain and need ...'

Brigit placed the coffee pot on the table just as

Peter appeared, dressed in jumper and jeans and bearing a cheery smile.

'You're looking more *beautiful* than ever, Brigit,' he said, kissing her on the cheek as he sat down.

'You're looking much *brighter*,' she added, pouring the coffee. 'Got your old glow back.'

'How about a walk after breakfast. I can show you the oak grove, and maybe a stroll round the lake if you're up to it?'

'I'd love to.' Brigit spooned porridge into her mouth. 'We can cook up the soup later if you like, when we get back.'

'Sounds like a *wonderful* plan.'

Later, the two friends left the house.

From beneath the porch, Peter picked up the shillelagh but stood a moment gazing over at the gatepost. His eye wandered along the fence line, past the hibiscus, then up the garden path to the apple tree.

Brigit looked at Peter, seeing him rapt in thought.

'I'll give you a penny for them,' she said, tousling her scarf about her neck.

117

'Oh, it's nothing really,' he said, half-smiling and casting another half-look to the post. 'Just that ... I've been seeing an owl hanging about here, over on that gate by the fence. Strange thing—it would just sit and stare at me, as if expecting something.' He turned to Brigit; his face lit with wonder. 'Last night, a strong wind woke me, and I got up to close the window. Gazing out to the garden, I saw the fox I told you about, standing right under that apple tree.' Peter pointed the shillelagh towards the garden wall. 'It stood completely still, looking right at me, knowing I was there at the window, and began to bark, like he was talking to me.'

Brigit glanced down the path then back at Peter, searching out his emerald eyes, as if trying to fathom the scope of his imagination.

"I must have been sound asleep ... I heard nothing," said Brigit, with an air of disbelief, and took Peter's arm and coaxed him to walk beside her as they crossed the drive.

Passing by the gatepost, Peter slowed a pace, pondering a moment on the idea that fox and owl might somehow share a common link. Immediately disregarding such fancy, he led Brigit out onto the lane.

They crossed the narrow bridge, taking the footpath along the hedged fields. With the sun warming the track, the clay had dried in hard, moulded ridges. The two friends walked single file under the shade of alder and ash, having the humming of hedge crickets for company.

Down the slope they strolled, and Peter took Brigit by the hand as they came to the riverbank, guiding her carefully across the fallen aspen that spanned the river. Midway between the banks, they stood captivated by the spectacular colours from the steady fall of autumn leaves that patterned the water.

Crossing the stream, they entered the quiet grove. Peter picked an oak leaf followed by those of hawthorn and ash, handing them to Brigit, showing her their unique patterns and similarities. Enamoured by his sheer love of nature, she took his arm once more as they strolled through the woods.

By the green margin of water, they sat and looked out across the peaceful lake. The last of the summer dragonflies darted above the sedge and rushes. The mother moorhen with her chicks came paddling by. Peter thrust his hand, pointing out to

Brigit the tiny tree growing on the rocky isle, describing to her how it appeared through the mist. 'Like a great sword, jutting up from the murky depths!' He put his arm around her waist as she rested her head gently on his shoulder.

It was late afternoon, and after returning to the house and filling their bellies with bowls of soup, Peter lay sleeping on the sofa.

Brigit's half-packed knapsack lay on the kitchen table. Shouldering the wall, she spoke quietly into the telephone.

'Thank you, Constable McCabe.' She listened and nodded her head. 'No, not too serious. Strangely, not a bump or bruise, but suffering with concussion, I'm sure. A blow like that, to the back of the head, could easily kill someone.' There was a long silence.

'Yes, he did. He said there were at least three of them, two crawling in the bushes, one came up from behind and struck him.'

Stepping from the kitchen, stretching the telephone cord and looking into the lounge, Brigit could see Peter was still asleep on the sofa. Just as she turned back to the kitchen, he opened his eyes.

'All I'm asking is you keep a lookout. I have to return to the city this evening and I would like some peace of mind knowing someone is watching over Hope House for a few days.' Brigit pressed her hand against her cheek. 'Thank you, Constable McCabe, for understanding.' She hung the phone back on the wall and stood gazing out of the window.

From the apple tree, Rudhek Robin broke out with cheerful rills.

Ghostwood stood silent. No wind stirred the tree-tops, neither rook nor crow flitted among the branches, not a creature moved beneath the brake.

Bathed in a single shaft of sunlight, Anam's body lay rigid. He was neither asleep nor injured—it was dread that bound him to the ground.

'Anam!' Dru's eerie shriek resounded, 'Anam.'

Slowly he stirred and opened his eyes. A kaleidoscopic swirl of shadowy shapes, irregular and amorphous, played about his blurry vision. Gradually the outline of trees and fern came into focus and his world restored.

Again, Dru was calling: 'Anam, you are in no immediate danger, but you must crack the shell of fear that binds you. Push through as though emerging from the egg again.'

Anam flexed his wings, feeling the blood rush to his flight muscles. Ruffling his feathers, he shuffled to his feet, tottering, as though standing for the first time, newly hatched into the world.

Ghostwood appeared much like any other wood—nothing like the terrible tales told by clan and tribe. The trees stood strangely silent, void of common bird call, yet there was a majestic air about their towering columns. The pines grew with such surety and strength; straight and stalwart to the sky. Where there were irregular areas of growth, sunlight penetrated the canopy, bringing wide green patches of fern to the forest floor.

Anam started running, stirring the dry pine needles with his beating wings. Finally, he was airborne and with renewed instinct for flight blazed through the woods, dashing deftly between the trees, turning and twisting, up to the loftier branches, higher and higher.

Swift as an arrow let free, Anam shot from the dark canopy into the bright light of day. Over the woods he soared, dropping into the gully on the far side, descending in a wide sweeping curve down into the valley.

Following Awen River, the waters thundered over the rocky ledges, and he welcomed the cool spray washing dust from his face and feathers. Onwards he coursed, to the crest of the sheep-specked hills.

Passing along the avenue of elms, now in their final flare of colour, he swept low over the meadowlands, and with brisk wingbeats and wavering glides, arrived at the ancient oak.

Dru was waiting. He welcomed Anam with open wings.

'It is time to unite,' declared Dru. 'No longer are we to be separated by species. Every clan, every tribe, must come together under the doctrine of kinship.'

Anam followed Dru into the hollow of the oak.

'I have spoken with Sion,' said Dru. 'The newcomer is our much-anticipated event. This human is a friend of nature, here to help us in our pain and need.' Lurching, the barn owl lowered his head. 'Fireun will help unite all animals, he will bring peace and harmony back to our troubled land.' In an instant, Dru disappeared out of the hollow, flying off to a far-reaching bough. Anam followed speedily, settling down next to him among the stalks of golden acorns.

'The heart of the earth gives life to all things,' Dru announced. 'There is a pulse throbbing through every leaf, every flower and every tree; all creatures, great and small, are enlivened by the same rhythms.'

Anam's heart overflowed with joy on hearing such wise words. He wanted to sing; he wanted to fly; he wanted to dance across the sky; but he sat quietly and composed and listened dutifully to all that Dru foretold.

The old owl taught the young owl all about the Fireun prophecy and the coming together of every clan and tribe. There would be a great battle and much courage needed in order to beat the stealers at their own game. 'What troubles come, can be overcome,' said Dru, watching as Tom Titmouse fluttered overhead, swooping and dashing at a buzzard, driving it away from his home range.

Dru and Anam talked until the sun passed its zenith.

Finally, Anam raised a personal question. 'Dru, what do I do about Otus? He doesn't want to see me ever again. I feel our relationship is fractured and can't be healed. I know he can be a bad-tempered, crotchety old owl, but ... pierce his prickly exterior and there is a heart both warm and true inside. He raised me, Dru, after my mother and father were struck down by the thunderfire. He taught me everything: how to fly, how to glide, swoop and dive. But our friendship is broken, and I feel I am to blame.'

Dru draped his mute-specked wing around Anam. 'As you do great work, you will become an inspiration to others. When Otus sees how you embrace hope, strength and courage, so shall the veil of his own pride and ignorance fall away. All animals must awaken and learn to follow their hearts. Fox and rabbit will live as friends; stoat and shrew may share their sacredness ... and a little owl shall lead them.' Dru gave a loud drawn-out shrill: 'Go now, do what you must do.'

Dru watched Anam lean into the breeze and lift gently off the bough, rising effortlessly, as if the wind alone picked him up and carried him away. Above the great oak he ascended, higher and higher, growing smaller and smaller, until he disappeared into the blue.

Anam gazed into the glittering waters of Awen River, following its windings back through the sun-filled valley. The lay of the land, the trees and rocks, the moving patterns of clouds reflecting in the pools, took on a new light. His whole world seemed clearer, sharper, more defined. He turned wide, yawing over the vast expanse of Ghostwood, knowing beneath its dark, doleful exterior was a world of serene beauty. Onward he flew, over the ridge, following the length of stone wall.

The sun was lowering, the day coming to a close when Anam reached Coll Spring. He came to rest on Ferne Stone and waited for Sion.

After placing the painting in the back of the car, Peter and Brigit dashed out to the platform. With seconds to spare they bade their farewell in a loving embrace. The train guard checked his pocket watch—4.32. Peter's heart panged at hearing the long shrill of the whistle and leaned into Brigit's body, feeling her breath against his skin. He held her tight, not wanting to let her go. Brigit kissed him on the lips and slipped gracefully from his arms up into the carriage.

From the window she leaned out and waved as

the train began to trundle.

'Goodbye, P. J. Goodhope! Try and stay out of any more trouble!'

'Fare thee well, Miss Dannan!' he yelled back. 'Visit again soon.'

He stood waving, watching the carriage curve round the bend until it disappeared. Alone on the platform, looking down the empty tracks, he took a long breath and let out a deep sigh before starting back to the car.

The limestone ticket office was aglow in the afternoon sun. Green railings tipped with red spiralling finials bordered a bed of yellow roses. He paused to pick a single flower, slipping the boutonniere inside the lapel of his jacket.

Spirit of Sion

Peter slipped a sheet of paper into the typewriter, hovered his hands above the keytop, and hoped for a flash of inspiration. He sat and waited. Drank some coffee. Contemplated the blank page. But no ideas came. The room filled with the steady beat of the longcase clock; a hollow sound that seemed to grow louder and choke the air. Swirling his cup, downing the dregs, he rose from the desk.

Knowing distraction often nourishes imagination, Peter ambled over to the bookcase, pulled out *The Ogham Tree Alphabet* and, sitting back at the desk, began leafing through its rubbed and dog-eared pages. The book told of an ancient language, steeped in mystery of unknown origin. The Ogham alphabet was the foundation to one of the early Celtic languages. Certain scholars believed that the names of various trees were ascribed to each individual marking or 'letter'. Simple strokes were notched into a 'menhir', an upright or 'standing' stone set in the ground vertically. Standing stones were purposely positioned, scattered across the countryside and used to write messages on for 'secret communication between the tribes', telling of ancestry, myth and magic. Captivated, Peter turned the page of the book. A 'druim', meaning 'stem', was first carved into the stone; a long vertical line running from bottom to top, sometimes using the natural edge of the rock as the stem. Other times the line ran horizontal, mainly when writing manuscripts. To the stem, one to five strokes were engraved, called 'flescs' or 'twigs', where each made up a single letter known as a 'fid', meaning 'tree'. Letters that formed words were known as 'fedas', meaning 'woods'. He liked the idea that words originated from the woods. *Wood-words.*

Slipping on his glasses, turning to the scribal desk and picking up his gold-nibbed pen, Peter began marking down each fid of the Ogham alphabet:

┬ ╥ ╥ ╥ ╥
┴ ╨ ╨ ╨ ╨
╀ ╫ ╫ ╫ ╫
┿ ╂ ╫ ╫ ╫

Next he listed the names of each tree, their corresponding Ogham names, letters and fids:

Tree	Ogham	Letter	Fid
Birch	Beith	B	┬
Rowan	Luis	L	╥
Alder	Ferne	F	╥
Willow	Saille	S	╥
Ash	Nuin	N	╥
Hawthorn	Huath	H	┴
Oak	Dair	D	╨
Holly	Tinne	T	╨
Hazel	Coll	C	╨
Apple	Queirt	Q	╨
Blackberry	Muin	M	╀
Ivy	Gort	G	╫
Broom/Fern	Ngetal	Ng	╫
Blackthorn	Straif	Z	╫
Elder	Ruis	R	╫

Pine/Fir	Ailm	A	+
Furze/Gorse	Onn	O	‡
Heather	Úr	U	⧺
Aspen	Edad	E	⧻
Yew	Idad	I	⧼

After working the entire alphabet, Peter scribed his own Ogham inscription:

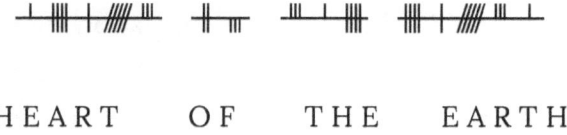

HEART   OF   THE   EARTH

He continued reading, biding the time, occasionally glancing over at the Imperial and its empty page waiting to be filled.

Closing the book, he started sorting idly through a loose pile of nuts, seeds and stones laying on the desk that he had collected on his walks. Casually he singled out a hag stone—a small piece of flint that had a hole worn through it—and, raising the stone to his eye, peered through the hole at the typewriter. Keeping himself amused, he next picked up a hazelnut and, taking his penknife to it, scratched into the shell a small stem followed by four flescs that represented Coll, the fid for the hazel tree, transforming the nut into an amulet—a charm that could invoke the spirit of the tree and so bring about a 'spark of inspiration; divinatory and visionary', or so he had just read. Time for a dram of Laphroaig to complete the ceremony.

Taking up the pen again, he began to draw the face of a fox, a quick sketching to keep his mind occupied and further pass the time, knowing inspiration would strike when least expected. An hour slipped past and, after two more drawings, he poured himself another drink.

Relaxing back in his chair, he turned to doodling, this time letting his hand do all the thinking. A squiggle evolved into a triple vesicae piscium; three intersecting ellipses that formed a triquetra; one continuous line interweaving around itself with no beginning or end. He'd read that Celtic trinity knots were often found engraved on ancient stone monuments. Scribbling more, shifting the contours, shading in the spaces, he transformed the leaf-like shape into a plain-looking shamrock. Peter flicked an eye at the Imperial. It now dawned on him that his ploy to ignite the *imbus*, the creative fires, was not happening. Setting down his pen, savouring the single malt and slapping his lips, Peter abandoned all work and play. He eased himself out the chair and walked up to the window.

Beyond the row of sycamores, a tractor was harrowing the slopes with scrapping seagulls trailing behind in their bid for an easy feed churned up by the plough. Above Ghostwood, a rabble of rooks were returning to roost. And along the rise came a brazen ringing of bells. It was the liturgy of the hour, the church calling to its flock. All seemed commonplace and constant. Then Peter looked down at the driveway. Anam landed swiftly onto the gatepost. Anam didn't stay long; he preened a short time, turned, and looked up at Peter with a peculiar stare, then hurriedly took to the air.

As Peter continued to stare at the vacant post, he recalled the words of the fox—the calling he had heard beneath his bedroom window: 'You are the one ... you are the one ...' kept repeating, rolling and tumbling in his mind, just like the peal of bells on the hillside, and he couldn't get the words out of his head.

He sat again, resting his elbows on the desk, meditating on the paper coiled in the typewriter. Dropping his chin in his hands, he continued to stare at the blank page waiting for *awen*, for inspiration to start flowing.

'Fireun, you are the one ... save us from the stealers ... save us from the stealers ...' clanged the bell in his brain.

The voice in his head suddenly stopped. The church bells fell silent. The room filled once more with the steady cadence of the clock.

Peter jumped in panic when the telephone rang.

Rushing up to cross the room, he had a sudden need to reach for the armchair to steady himself, as if his legs might fail him, as if the ground beneath his feet had started to pitch and roll like the sea. His head felt heavy as a rock, vision swimming, and a high-pitched sound screamed through his ears as he collapsed into the chair.

The telephone went silent.

The room stopped swaying.

Gradually he released his grip on the armrest and took a deep breath.

Feeling the need for open air, he heaved himself

up from the chair and went lumbering into the hall. Lifting the latch, he opened the door—Sion Fox was sitting on the step. Peter was neither shocked nor surprised, only spellbound by the animal's bold, unwavering presence. Entranced, he felt his spirit being drawn, absorbed into those amber bewitching eyes.

'Fireun, you are the one,' said the fox. 'Save us from the stealers,' he barked.

In an instant, Peter dropped to the ground on hands and knees—yet no longer was he by the door-step of his house, but in woodland, among trees and ferns, slinking on all fours, feeling the damp peat beneath his paws. A chestnut tree stood high on a mound, broad and tall, and beneath the trunk was a large hole, a burrow, which he found himself scur-rying down underground, following the twists and turns of tunnels. There came a light at the end of a winding passage leading out to a rocky outcrop. Feel-ing the sun warm upon his back, he curled himself up beneath Ferne Stone, face nuzzling into his red bushy tail.

A zephyr stirred an eddy of leaves washing over Peter's face. Opening his eyes, he was back on the doorstep of his house. The fox was gone, the evening drawn, and the only sound was the whirring wings of mallards as they flew low across the twilit sky heading for the lake.

Was it a dream, a vision, some crazy imagining? Sauntering down to the gatepost, Peter gazed out at the sycamores silhouetted against the evening sky and began to wonder if he'd ever really seen the fox; that maybe the owl was also a creature of his own conjuring. *Surely the whole idea of talking animals was a complete and utter fantasy?* Out from the crepuscular landscape came a distant yip of fox followed by the quavering cry of a little owl.

Just as he was starting back to the house, Peter noticed a faint light flickering out on the far edge of the field, moving slowly along the line of sycamores. Poised, he watched with fierce attention the intermittent light swinging back and forth. Tilting his head to one side, his senses grew keen, and he could hear the low rustling of feet stomping down the grass, sticks breaking underfoot ... the chafe of a man's cough. Across the darkening skyline came two toiling figures carrying a torch, trudging their way between the trees heading straight for the ridge.

'Stealers!'

GhosTwood

Like the wind, Peter raced to the house, threw on his coat, snatched the torch from the table and grabbed the shillelagh. Dashing across the drive, with one hand hinging off the gatepost, he sprang clear over the fence.

Once inside the perimeter of the field, Peter's perspective suddenly changed. 'The hunter now the hunted,' he whispered, every nerve throbbing in his body. With a low-to-the-ground stalking posture, he made off for the shadow of the hedgerow.

Peter was surprised at how he was able to perceive the murky landscape merely by starlight. With the gift of keen sight, he could clearly make out two ghostly figures halfway across the margin of field ahead of him. Lifting his nose, questing the air, he detected the spoor of stealers; the stench of sweat and cigarette smoke. Looking back, the faint glow of Hope House seemed of a sudden to belong to another world. Thunderclouds came bearing up from the south, widening upwards from the horizon, snuffing out the stars.

Now and then a rabbit would cross Peter's path, or a roosting bird stirred in the hedgerow, but such surprises only sharpened the senses and helped preserve his vigilance. Quietly over the turf he trod, tracking the flickering light, edging closer towards the north ridge.

Leaving the field, Peter squeezed through a breakage in the boundary wall and pushed up the steep gorge, his heart beating fast and strong. Using the shillelagh to steady him, he came out onto the north ridge. He saw the poacher's light dip down then disappear into a hedging of blackthorn. Only a barrier of briar stood between him and Ghostwood. A look of unease came over Peter as he gazed up at the dark trees that dwarfed him. The white of his eye betrayed his fear. For a second, Peter was young again, six years old and scared of ghosts.

Merlyn Blackbird chittered nervously inside the briar as Peter drew near the woods. Then the bird shrilled its alarum.

Bealert! Bealert! Bealert!

Peter clicked on his torch, shading the light through the narrow slits of his fingers, and, taking a deep breath for courage, with head bent, he shouldered through the thorny branches; branches that to him appeared like monstrous limbs, like the bones of claws.

No more than ten yards away there came a small clearing. Peter could see one of the stealers; he was shining a hunting light high into the canopy of the forest. The other had his back to him, pointing a gun right where the light was cast, ready to take a bird on the bough. 'They're lamping!' Peter whispered, switching off his torch. He watched as the spotlight scanned about the upper branches. Slowly and silently Peter advanced, slipping behind one tree, then another, quietly closing in on his prey.

A shot was fired, the muffled sound of an air rifle—*a .22 calibre rook rifle*, thought Peter.

Another shot fired; this time followed by a loud

clatter of wings where several birds stirred restively from their roost-tree. The light honed in on a single crow that suddenly took to wing, flapping wildly as it began jumping blindly between the branches, causing further panic among the flock. The light swung his way—Peter crouched beneath the bracken. The poacher's light switched off, casting the woods into total blackness. For a while the crows continued to caw and flap their wings. Then the birds began to settle and soon a deathly silence filled the dark. Waist-high among the ferns, Peter kept perfectly still and waited.

The hunter's light flicked back on followed by quick gunfire, setting off a jabbering of birds. Soft-footed through the brushwood, Peter inched forward. He heard muted voices just ahead. Less than five yards from the huntsmen, he suddenly felt the cold touch of a bony hand reach for the back of his neck. He stopped, gripped by fear, recalling the innkeeper's words of warning: *Whoever be unfortunate to behold that ghostly figure on a moonless night shall, with cold-curdling scream, vanish without a trace.* Slowly he turned, hoping not to come face-to-face with the ghost of a murderer. One gentle tug of the blackthorn freed him from the snag that had hooked the hood of his coat.

Again, a rifle shot. A scurrying of feet came brushing through the scrub.

Peter ducked down, deeper into the dense thicket. On all fours he crawled between the fibrous stalks, having now the advantage of being able to observe yet remain unseen. With the poacher's light illuminating the treetops, Peter peered up between the sprays of leaves. Hearing their harsh protesting cries, he could see the black shapes of birds flitting fearfully from tree to tree.

'Don't waste time with the rook-rifle, Fenning,' came a hushed voice, 'Use the barrel. You might even kill two birds with one shot!'

A wide gap appeared between the brake. Peter needed to get closer. He made a dash for the next covering.

'Over there, Fenn!' came a gruff shout. 'Shoot from there!'

A dark figure strode brusquely through the undergrowth towards Peter. Hearing the fleshy stalks breaking underfoot, Peter flopped belly-down, keeping a tight grip on the shillelagh while the hunter's light swept over him. Laying deep among the fronds, Peter found himself staring at a pair of muddy wading boots and the barrel end of a shotgun. Too busy looking up at the trees, Fenning did not see Peter lying there embosked beneath the bracken.

Peter watched powerlessly as one of the crows flew to a neighbouring tree, caught in the spotlight. It flapped its wings frantically, jumping bough to bough. The poacher took a careful aim and fired—the flash and report together brought Feannag Crow tumbling down in a rain of twigs, thudding to the ground next to the poacher, who stuffed the bird inside a sack and slung it over his shoulder.

'Good shot, Fenn,' laughed Morgan, shining the light into his face. 'But enough of these crazy crows; that's all we seem to be catching tonight.'

'Dearg says we need diversity,' Fenning replied, opening the barrel and emptying the chamber of its spent cartridge. 'Let's head back to the ridge, we might get lucky and bag ourselves an owl or two.'

The smell of sulphur lingered from the gunfire. Peter lay motionless beneath the ferns while the men stole off through the woods. Poking his head up, seeing the poachers were a fair distance, he continued to stalk them.

There came a loud shouting, a guffawing. Peter closed in on the two men. They were brazenly kicking in a large burrow in the ground.

'Don't see badgers round here anymore,' Fenning spat.

'Perhaps they've all gone to greener pastures.' Morgan stood and rolled a cigarette.

'Come to think of it, haven't really seen a single animal about these woods for weeks now,' added Fenning, 'just a bunch of bloody rooks and crows.' He began stomping about on the ground, collapsing in the galleries and main tunnel.

'We should go hunting further afield.' Morgan lit his cigarette. 'Maybe tomorrow night we take a look over by Ferne Stone. I'm pretty sure that's where we'll find that old wily fox hiding. Let's set him a trap.' Morgan spewed a cloud of cigarette smoke while snuffing out the match.

The men strode on, following a set of rutted tracks. Peter followed, sliding between the tree trunks.

Eventually, the two men stepped out of the

woods, heading east towards the rise. Peter saw them milling about the Bedford van parked a short way up on the verge. Staying under the protective cover of the woods, he kept a safe watch. He would strike when the moment was right. When the men were disarmed and distracted. He would use the cudgel end of the shillelagh if he had to.

Headlights appeared in the distance. A vehicle veered at the stone wall up at the lane, turning onto the dirt track, bouncing along towards the woods.

Peter slipped behind a tree and waited.

The approaching headlights drew near. A police car pulled up beside Morgan and Fenning as they made ready to leave with their spoils.

'Evening, lads, good catch tonight?'

'Evening, Constable McCabe,' said Morgan, doffing his hat. 'We got you a nice brace of plump pheasants for the pot. Still no luck with snaring a partridge—but how about a couple of fat conies to keep the wife happy?' Morgan turned and gave Fenning a sly wink, jerking his head in the direction of the van.

McCabe was a burly bearded man almost too big to fit in the car. Clambering out he stood with a beady stare, scanning the woods before opening the car boot. Peter watched as Fenning passed Morgan a brace of rabbits from the back of the Bedford, followed by two pheasants wrapped in sacking. Morgan placed the animals inside the back of the police car. Slamming the boot lid and with mutual handshakes, the deed was done. The men exchanged no further words as they each climbed into their vehicles.

With the quarry gone to ground, the hunt was over.

McCabe turned the car around and headed back along the winding track followed by the Bedford, bucking and backfiring.

Leaving the woods behind, Peter started home towards the stone wall, watching the lights of the Bedford and police car move further away over the rise. There came a few large raindrops pattering his shoulder then all at once a thunderbolt raked the sky. With a loud thunderclap, the clouds opened in a great flood that filled the tracks, washing the earth over the ridge in a stream of muddy water. Pulling the hood over his head, Peter bowed against the driving rain.

Arriving home on the chime of midnight, wet, weary and disheartened, Peter was in need of a hot bath. He kicked off his wet boots under the porch and duly hung the shillelagh by the door and went inside the house.

First Gathering

Sion stood on Ferne Stone looking down over the assembly of animals. Many had gathered, some relinquishing their resting period to attend the meeting. An atmosphere of apprehension and quiet desperation hung in the air.

Sion studied their faces, their body language. Some sitting, others standing, segregated into groups according to family or species. To his left, voles, dormice and shrews huddled under a rock, nervous of nearby predators. Dobran Otter stood to his right; a deep sadness expressed in his wide brown eyes. Up on a protruding stone, half-coiled, Nathair Snake was flicking her tongue out, tasting the air. There was Elan Hare, sitting in form, watching Greynog Hedgehog roll into a prickly ball as a group of baby rabbits came hopping by in playful banter, harkening to every sound with noses twitching.

In the middle of the clearing stood a gang of rowdy weasels, jeering at their quarry, hissing, shrilling, sometimes letting out a high-pitched *Yac!*—making the insectivores, peering from under their rock, ever wary. With fitful gazes, the little rabbits kept their distance, but a clan of badgers heeded not the weasels' unruly behaviour. They only looked upon the rapscallion creatures with cynical expressions.

Silent and aloof, three raptors, Bod Osprey, Gavina Hawk and Hok Falcon sat high in the ash tree, curiously observing the meeting while Kasek Woodpecker and Cruidín Kingfisher perched together on the hawthorn, wind-blown against the hillock.

Around Coll Spring, the hazels were filling up with noisy sparrows and down among the crags and crevices, Rudhek Robin and Dreean Wren went splashing through the rills, washing their wings beneath the gentle falls.

Then in came the latecomers; the ravens, the rooks and the crows, cawing constantly as they circled above.

'Fellow friends ... former enemies ... thank you for attending.' Sion spoke softly. The crowd settled and looked up at the fox on the rock. 'It seems more and more are coming to a greater understanding, a deeper realisation, that what happens to one animal affects all animals. We are in the midst of a great calamity, one that threatens our very existence.' All chattering ceased. The rabbits stopped hopping, the weasels finished short of jostling with Greynog Hedgehog, who had unfortunately rolled into their camp.

'Our gathering today is a call for action,' continued Sion, 'an invitation for all to join us on a quest to restore peace among our kind in accordance with the prophecy spoken of by Dru Barn Owl.'

After the crow family had finally settled down in the crown of the rowan, not a single creature stirred. A hundred pairs of eyes fixed on Sion.

'Last night, Feannag Crow was taken from her roost at Ghostwood,' Sion gravely announced. 'She was brought down with the thunderfire. Rhea and

Druantia Pheasant are still missing from Muin Lane, where the thunderfire was also heard during the dark hours. Hope is dwindling for Ostara Rabbit and her mate, last seen at dusk crossing the north ridge.'

The animals looked round at one another, anxious of the news but perhaps more troubled by the abnormal aggregation of so many creatures amassed in one place. The raptors appeared proud and noble, confident that each could fend for themselves. Some woodpigeons, however, were nervous, appeared befuddled, leaping from branch to branch. Others strutted the ground, bowing and fanning their tails, not knowing whether to stay or take leave. The weasels started up their usual ranting, evidently unmoved by the report, mocking the crowd again, hissing at any who dared come near. But a few attendees, each of different tribes and clans, moved a little closer, sharing a mutual concern.

Sion continued, 'I have noted the locations of many bonebreakers. Alas, we cannot outsmart the thunderfire.' The animals stirred, muttering nervously among themselves.

'Anam and I have recently made contact with a human believed to be Fireun. Dru Barn Owl informs us that never before in the history of our kingdom has such animal-to-human communication taken place.' The animals looked at each other with curiosity then eyed Sion with deep suspicion. 'Anam will conclude the initiation; he will help Fireun cross the threshold that divides our world with the world of human.'

The notion of letting a human enter their realm sent a wave of fear through the gathering. A great raucous soon erupted. The birds began to flap their wings nervously, unhinged at the thought of beastly man entering their domain. They looked warily at Sion.

Brogan Badger stepped away from his clan, peering down his banded nose at the hodgepodge of animals. He knew all too well the nature of humans, especially stealers. He himself bore the mark of a shot hole through his right ear—a narrow escape from the thunderfire one summer eve on returning to his den. Brogan coughed and snorted as he sauntered off, mumbling beneath his breath something along the lines of how it was all a complete waste of time. But a few creatures nudged a little nearer, forming a circle around Ferne Stone, each conversing among their kind, speaking in their native tongues.

Anam came down from the alder, landing next to Sion on the stone platform.

Kiew-kiew! Kiew-kiew! Anam yipped, hoping to silence the ceaseless chatter. 'Please ... listen ... all of you. Gather closer. Try and speak in the ancient language, so we may all understand.'

The animals looked perplexed. Some appeared cynical, chary of their host, others plain indifferent. Bird and beast came face to face, agreeing, disagreeing, their arguing rising into a riotous gabble.

Anam gave another loud screech: 'No single tribe can solve this problem alone. Dru says we need to come together as one. There is strength in unity. Dru says to put aside our differences. We have to change our common ways of thinking if we are to survive these troubling times.' He lowered his tone. 'Together we prevail, divided we fail. Doing nothing, turning a blind eye, will ultimately lead to our extinction.' The animals studied Anam and Sion standing together.

'When we are gathered, we are strong,' added Sion.

The company turned and considered one another, wondering if it were at all possible to see eye to eye. Hazel Dormouse, a comely creature, peered out from under her rock and looked up at Bronwen Weasel. She wanted desperately to see Bronwen as her ally, not her enemy, and cast her a timid smile. But the weasel only snarled back at her.

Kiew-kiew, cried Anam. 'Fireun has already received the spirit of Sion. Soon he shall see the world through the eyes of an owl—then he will be one of us.' Anam looked over the gathering. He could tell they were afraid. He could see allowing man into their world was sacrilege.

'Humans are cursed,' growled Sion, strategically taking the side of the animals. 'They have the ability to take actions not constrained by the codes of nature. They have hewed the earth and plundered its bounty. Their free will is an abomination when used for selfish gain. Greed swells the stomach, blights the owner, breeds suspicion, fear, and hatred, and always, always, ends in—WARH! WARH! WARH!' Sion barked, scornfully. The animals looked on in cold silence.

'But one stands out from the rest—one human

alone in the wilderness of hope.' Sion looked hard into the faces of every animal. 'Fireun is our friend. He shares in the fate of all of us,' Sion concluded.

The animals started up prattling again. Approving, disapproving, agreeing, disagreeing; they were confused, angry, scared and disturbed by what their world was becoming.

'You may think allowing man into our world seems foolish and fraught with danger.' Sion spoke soberly. 'And the idea of us coming together as one family sounds outlandish.' Fox and owl gazed at the creatures that in recent past were their quarry. Hazel Dormouse slipped back beneath her rock, safe in the company of vole and shrew. 'But we cannot fight wickedness in a land divided. We animals must band together; friend with foe, kin and rival, for what happens to one affects the other.'

Anam took a deep breath, 'It doesn't matter whether you are born of the strigid or canid clan, murid or any of the tribes of mustelid, we are all connected, each of us a branch of the same tree of life, all belonging to the earth.' Anam hunched forward, craning his head. 'Adopt Fireun into your family—he is our one chance of survival. He is our only hope.'

There was a quiet air of calm. Not a breath of wind, not a single creature sounded on the hill.

Anam glanced at Sion; they sensed hostility, a simmering resistance amid the horde. A rabbit and stoat stood strangely eyeing each other. Birds began to flitter from bough to bough.

Sion spoke out to the restive mob: 'If you feel what we say rings true in your heart, step forward, join us. Anam and I offer you the bond of friendship and family, sanctuary for all.'

Bronwen Weasel was the first to break the silence. She let out a piercing scream and scurried off, cursing and snarling before disappearing under the furze. One by one the animals parted. Elan Hare loped away, hop by hop, heading home for the fields. Connyn Rabbit gathered up his kits and scampered off across the hillside. Flapping restlessly, all the birds took off at once, heading in different directions.

The autumn wind blew the dry leaves, driving them over the ground.

Crestfallen, Anam and Sion stood staring at the vacant earth. The wind gave a last heave through the hazels ... then a deathly hush.

A spritely squirrel came leaping from the branches of one of the hazel trees. Spiralling down the trunk, she sprinted towards them.

'Hello, Anam, hello, Sion,' she trilled, her red tail flagging high and quivering. 'Don't look so glum,' she squeaked. 'Let them go away and think about it. You've sown the seed of hope, that's a good start!'

Anam and Sion looked curiously at the lively creature.

'I'd love to join your good company,' the squirrel chirped, sitting beside them on the stone slab. 'I've lost my whole family. Many more of my kind have been stolen. So scared have I been, I hid myself in the meadowlands beyond the valley—to be as far away from the stealers as possible. I heard from Dru you were coming today, to help gather us together, so I left at dawn to be here. My name is Cara.'

'Welcome, Cara,' said Sion, raising his paw.

'You know Dru Barn Owl?' asked Anam. Intrigued, Anam moved closer to Cara.

'Oh, yes,' answered the squirrel. 'Dru and I have spent many a rainy day sheltering in the hollow, contemplating the fate of our world. He foretold everything about you and Sion becoming friends—he spoke of this special event even back in the spring-time.' Cara stood up on her hind legs. 'Dru says we each have a responsibility for bringing hope to every creature in the land.'

Anam gave a happy jiggle, thrilled to be acquainted with their first real ally.

Sion, Anam and Cara talked for the remainder of the day. They shared their knowledge on how all living things are allied to the bond of nature that connects everything to the world. They pledged they would find a way to unite the animals, to prepare them for their skirmish against the stealers. Anam felt comfort in knowing a new friend had joined them on their quest for peace.

In the fading light they huddled on the stone, agreeing to meet again, after Fireun had been fully initiated into the animal realm. As the stars began to shine so the company parted each their separate ways.

Sion lay beneath the stone table to sleep where the earth was still warm from the afternoon sun. Cara scurried back to the ring of hazels, to rest and gather energy for her journey home to the meadowlands.

Following the curve of the stone wall, Anam decided he would sleep at Beith Barn until the moon had risen. He alighted on the rafter; eyes heavy with sleep. It had been a long, exhausting day. He gazed down at Lugh Wood Mouse scurrying under the hay cart, carrying an ear of barley. Anam closed his eyes. His mind was on Cara, and he began to dream of flying with her over meadows coloured with bell-flowers and bee orchids, swooping low, side by side along the sparkling waters of Awen River, soaring high above the peaceful valley ... Anam drifted off to sleep.

WaTcher of The Sky

The village clock tolled one.

Anam opened his eyes to the sound of scurrying feet in the darkness below. It was Lugh Wood Mouse again, collecting in stalks of wild oat, garnering the grain for the coming winter. Anam was hungry. He would need to eat soon, but not Lugh—he had a promise to keep.

Lugh stood up, whiskered nose quivering. Letting out a gentle squeak, he scampered from beneath the cart. Head cocked, beak open, Anam took to wing, his low sweeping shadow sending Lugh running for his life. Over the mouse he flew and out of the barn, breathing in the crisp night air, his mind brimming with happy thoughts of Sion and Cara.

Under the black swathe of night, the earth seemed a safe and unsullied place. Woods and vales appeared calm and serene, unvarying, and mysterious. How grateful Anam was for the gift of wings. He came low over the fields, undulating above the gleaming grass, talons down, wings outstretched, and landed swiftly upon the gatepost, letting out a happy hoot.

Peter jerked back from the typewriter letting out a jolly yip—'Woo-hoo!' He pulled the paper from the carriage and placed it on the mounting pile of pages.

From his perch, Anam could see the outline of Peter move up to the window.

Peter stood, folding his arms, gazing out towards the gatepost.

Anam braced himself as Peter moved away from the window and a moment later the door of the house creaked open. In the glow of the porch light, even from a distance, their eyes instantly met. Peter made his way across the drive down to the gate. He stopped a few feet from Anam, and for a quiet moment each gazed upon the other. There was an immediate sense of kinship, as if they knew each other from some long-forgotten past. A gentle breeze blew up from the field, just enough to stir feather and hair alike.

Stepping closer, Peter said, 'I feel I already know you, Anam Little Owl.' The owl blinked his big yellow eyes. 'But how is this possible?' Peter frowned, shaking his head. 'I don't understand.'

'You don't need to understand, Fireun—just go with it,' cheeped Anam with a playful nod. 'There is a pulse deep in the heart of the earth, a natural cadence which beats in all of us, connecting everything to everything: all creatures, all rivers, rocks and trees. The sun that lights the earth, the moon that lifts the tides, every star tempering the rhythms of life—all are moved by the same measure.'

Peter looked puzzledly at the owl then gazed dreamily up at the night sky. Like a joining of dots, a line of silver light seemed to etch across the dome, connecting all the stars, mapping out the firmament, and he could see clearly the constellations of Capricornus, Aquarius and Pisces, relative to the Great Square of Pegasus twinkling back from the black canvas.

'There, on the horizon, is Fomalhaut—the lonely star of autumn,' hooted Anam. 'It ushers in the fall of leaves, preparing all animals, instructing us to forage and hoard while winter draws near.'

For the first time Peter understood the stars, seeing them not only as systems of navigation used by man or beast, but markers that influenced the habits of all living things; when to seed, when to bear fruit, what time to bring forth young into the world or to gather in the harvest. It was like each star was part of the jewelled movement of some gigantic cosmic clock, maintaining order and forever constant and predictable. And when mapped together in constellation, the specks of light formed symbols, like the runes of some incredible alphabet.

Anam blinked again his big yellow eyes. 'In our realm, you are known as Fireun, watcher of the sky. Born of the light in the heavens.' Anam leaned forward on the post. 'Like the stars, we are each a radiant body filling the great void.' Peter kept his gaze upon the night sky, feeling drawn into that vast empire of space. Such was his vision fixed he became completely absorbed in those dizzying spectres of light—millions and millions, billions and billions of tiny white dots pinpricking the darkness. He felt a familiar light-headedness come upon him and began to lean as if the horizon had started to spin, and the ground fell away beneath his feet.

He did not fall, but instead found himself rising above the ground, flying—soaring like a bird. With a piercing shrill, Fireun flew over the rooftop of the house, his large open wings lifting him higher and higher up into the starry night.

He gazed at the world rushing beneath his body, looked up at the gigantic moon shining above the hills, watched his whole world turning whiter and brighter, until he became absorbed into that one great luminous orb. The light consumed him, stole away all form. And in that formless, spaceless void, the blinding whiteness began to drone, like a persistent echo. The sound grew louder. Clearer. Words formed. Spoken words. A voice was calling him from the light. A dull monotonous voice.

'Are you all right? Can you hear me?'

Peter opened his eyes, found himself propped against the gatepost, the light still burning his vision, and it wavered, as if under control by some invisible hand. Climbing to his feet, an apparition slowly appeared before him—the hazy outline of a police car.

'I'm Constable McCabe,' came the voice behind the light. 'Are you all right, sir?'

'Uh ... yes,' Peter mumbled, brushing the loose dirt from his sleeves. 'I must have slipped.' He took a deep breath to ground himself. A quick glance back at the post and Anam was gone.

McCabe turned the torchlight away from Peter's face, pointing it directly at the house.

Peter stepped up to the car. 'Good evening, Constable. My name is Peter Goodhope—I live here.'

'You say you slipped, sir?' asked McCabe, illuminating Mr Toad parked under the carport. 'Were you perhaps climbing over the fence?' He turned the torchlight onto the gatepost.

Peter winced at the policeman's veiled remark while at the same time puzzled over what had just happened—and where was Anam? Glancing at the vacant post, he said, 'I was out taking a walk before bed. Must have lost my balance, that's all. As I said, I live here: this is my home.'

McCabe turned the light back on Peter, officially eyeing him up and down. Peter felt uncomfortable under the policeman's silent scrutiny.

'Constable McCabe,' Peter broke the silence, 'have there been any recent reports of poaching about the village? Trappings of wild animals, shootings in the woods?'

McCabe shone the torch directly back onto Peter's face.

'Nothing of the kind, Mr Goodhope,' the policeman replied with a stern voice. 'Have you any reason to believe such a thing?' There followed another awkward silence.

Peter moved closer to the car, shading his face. 'I found an animal trap beneath some bushes, right here along the drive. Freshly baited.'

McCabe kept his steely cool. 'There have been no such reports,' he replied firmly. 'But rest assured, Mr Goodhope, I shall keep a sharp lookout. Probably kids.'

McCabe turned off the light. 'Well, looks like you're okay. Everything seems to be in order, just you be more mindful next time you go wandering about the middle of the night.'

Peter nodded, said nothing more and stepped back from the car. He watched as McCabe swung the vehicle round and disappeared down the drive.

Looking to the gatepost, Peter's gaze turned slowly up towards the night sky, at the sweep of twinkling stars.

Digging Out

The sun played upon the water—a sea of sequins sparkling silver.

Anam was relaxing in the willow, enjoying the sweet flesh of a crabapple, watching a dragonfly dart between the sedge grass, glinting in the sunshine as she came to rest on the tilt of a leafy blade. Home among the lilies, Losgann Frog slumbered by the reed bed. From out of the bulrushes, Cruidín Kingfisher skimmed the lake, leaving a memory of blue flashes as she plucked a minnow clean out of the water.

Full from his morning meal, Anam puffed out his feathers to keep himself warm.

Peter was at his easel working the canvas, applying strokes of radiant yellow, creating reflections of sunlight on the water beneath the willow that mantled the shore. Adding a few gold dabs highlighting the owl's face, he stepped back to admire the painting of Anam at home on Saille Lake.

The telephone rang.

'Hello,' Peter answered.

'Peter,' came a familiar voice, 'I've been thinking about you, missing you terribly.'

'Brigit! How are you?' He heard a loud buzzing on the line. 'Pardon? I can hardly hear you, what's all that noise?'

'I'm at the theatre,' shouted Brigit, 'backstage, with a crew of carpenters, electricians and designers, we're testing out the collapse of the windmill ... hang on a bit ...' The line went static for a moment. 'I'm on a five-minute break from rehearsals, so I have to make this a quick call.'

Peter peered out the kitchen window at the sun reflecting off Mr Toad's chrome headlamp. 'Looks like a nice day for a drive,' he said, more to himself than to Brigit.

'How's that poor head of yours?' she asked.

Running a hand down the back of his scalp, Peter felt something cold and squidgy between his fingers; a splodge of wet paint. 'Good as gold,' he laughed, and duly wiped his hand down his smock. 'What about you, how's life in the world of drama?'

The telephone went silent.

'Sorry, the director's started screaming again,' said Brigit in a low voice. 'I must get back to work. Must dash. I'll call you later in the week, though I'm not home much these days.' Resuming her normal tone, she added, 'So glad you're feeling better though. Just wanted to check in. Got to go. Bye!'

'Okay, thanks for the call, bye, Brigit.'

Peter waited for Brigit to hang up. He removed his smock and walked out along the passageway. Slipping on a jacket, he collected the car keys from the table and paused at the hall mirror. 'Lots of people talk to animals. Not very many listen though. That's the problem,' he cited to himself. Noticing a small smudge of yellow paint left across his brow, he promptly wiped it away with the pad of his finger. Adjusting the lay of his scally cap, Peter left the house.

It was a bright sunny morning driving into

Nemeton. Neighbours stood outside their rose-covered cottages exchanging news over white picket fences. Children played on the village green, turning cartwheels, chasing ducks to the pond.

Nemeton had been settled since historical records began, built on a plateau overlooking Awen River. The one cobbled road leading into the main town square had been worn smooth over centuries of hooves and wheels. Oak-beamed buildings lined the main street. A butcher, a baker, a cobbler, a tailor. But there was one particular place Peter had come to visit. He parked the car and looked up at the sign above the shop door.

MOST PECULIAR
Objet D'art
Purveyors of Old Curiosities & Rare Artefacts
PROPRIETOR: J. J. JAROME
ESTABLISHED 1792

A small bell tinkled above the door as Peter entered the building.

Projecting out on a driftwood plaque, a gruesome pike greeted him from the wall—a hostile show of its needle-teeth made out as if to strike. Next to the stuffed fish, Peter was met by a deer head. He winced, knowing the beautiful beast once grazed peaceful meadows. Making his way deeper into the murky emporium, Peter picked through a wicker basket full of ebonised walking canes, each stick capped with grotesque claw handles; embalmed grapplers and paws that had once belonged to rare and exotic animals of the tropics.

Peter studied curious carved figures housed in glass cabinets: a triad of dancing women interwoven into a trinity knot and a large statue of a goddess, warrior-cast, holding a crow above her brow. On a plinth there stood a wooden statue of a human with the head of a falcon.

He noticed other collectables of a more rustic theme: a man and boy holding rod and line. A rearing horse with huntsman astride, baying hounds at the heel. Two spaniel dog figurines, one carrying a duck seized in its mouth. A dozen or more die-cast otters, badgers, stoats and weasels, and hand-painted birds of every kind. And amidst the rural scene—a bronzed poacher clutching his gun.

Many-sized clocks ticked and droned their metallic sounds, key-wound and weight-driven. Springs whirred, hammers struck chime rods to the melodious sounds of St Michael's and Whittington.

Adorning one central wall were varicoloured masquerade masks detailing bizarre caricatures of rabbits and eagles, while on the opposite wall hung tribal heads of Africans and Aztecs, depicting bizarre human faces, some having horns, others bearing hideous beaks of birds.

Along the shop window, freestanding on a burled walnut coffer, stood a large stuffed animal, a mounted fox. It seemed to stare straight at Peter with a fixed, malevolent grin. Looking closely, he could see its captive—a rabbit trapped beneath its paw. The mount captured the moment between life and death, the act of killing. His heart quickened. The mimetic scene struck Peter as a mockery of the natural world.

Atop a rolltop desk Peter spotted an owl seated under a glass dome, its dull, imitative eyes staring off into space. Somewhere among the vulgar relics, a voice called out to him.

'Good afternoon, sir. Can I help you with anything?'

Peter turned, his eye cast towards a counter stacked high with large leather-bound books. There was a masthead lantern, several rolled maps and other maritime equipment taking up the rest of the desk. Then Peter saw him—an old man, his head poking out between a ship's brass bell and a diver's helmet. He could also make out the scrawny face of a tomcat peering at him over the rim of an antique terrestrial globe, peeking, as it were, above the Andes.

'Are you Jarome, the owner of the shop?' Peter called out to the man.

'Yes, indeed, sir,' the man replied. 'Sixth generation, last of the breed.' Behind thick-lensed spectacles, Jarome blinked eagerly. 'How may I help you today, sir?' he asked again.

Peter turned back to the stuffed owl and began to examine it more closely. The bird appeared old and rather bedraggled, its feathers frayed and lustreless. 'Can you tell me where this bird comes from? How old it is? How long you've had it in your shop?'

Jarome eased himself onto frail spindly legs and aided by a walking stick, tottered across the wooden floor.

'That, sir, comes from the Animalia Kingdom;

Strix aluco, commonly called a tawny owl.' Jarome coughed into a handkerchief and cleared his throat. 'I've had the piece sitting in the shop for nigh on seven years, so its age, at a guess, is probably close to twenty. A superb specimen, once a much-desired object, well preserved and professionally mounted. Originally one of a pair, but its partner I sold separately, about a year ago.'

Peter ogled the decrepit man now standing beside him. Already he disliked Jarome and didn't much care for his shop either—offended by the manner in which dead animals were seen as objects of desire.

'And the fox?' Peter pointed.

'*Vulpes vulpes*. Could be as old as thirty, sir. If not more.'

Peter turned to the man. 'Do you have any recently stuffed creatures, say over the last twelve months? Something a bit more ... fresh?'

Jarome peered over his spectacles. 'I'm afraid not, sir. All my mounts, including the pike and deer, are quite old. Taxidermy is a dying art.'

Peter ignored the weak witticism and gazed about the shop crammed with misplaced objects.

The air was sickly, thick with lignin; a suffocating smell of aging glue, perishing paper and old wood.

A grandmother clock struck its hammer on a coiled gong. As the chime echoed away, the slow ticking of the clock resumed, the sound almost mournful. Turning back to the shopkeeper, who himself appeared as old as time, Peter realised no further information was to be gleaned. Certainly not from any of the dusty artefacts. Peter was about to leave when a loud explosion sounded right outside the shop. Through the grimy window, Peter watched the Bedford van drive past, backfiring and chugging out clouds of thick smoke. Taking leave, Peter rushed to the door and dashed onto the street.

Glancing past the grimacing fox, Jarome peered out the shop window, seeing Peter speeding off in his car.

Keeping his distance, Peter followed the Bedford through the town along the cobbled street, then down the hill they sped. Crossing the packhorse bridge, the van pulled up outside the train station. Peter spied a cloaked figure appear from the van carrying two wooden boxes into the station. A moment later, the man reappeared and, climbing back into the Bedford, the pursuit continued.

On leaving Nemeton, short of a mile, the van veered down a dirt track. Peter slowed as he drove past the turn-off. He watched the back of the Bedford disappear behind a massive blackthorn bush. Through the overgrowth he spied a ramshackle farmhouse smothered with ivy.

ReTurn To GhosTwood

It was getting dark when Anam landed on the gatepost. He hooted softly and waited.

Peter stepped out beneath the porch light.

'I'm glad you're taking to this much easier, Fireun,' Anam called out. 'We don't have much time. Our world is in deepest peril. Only you can help put an end to our suffering and stop our lives from being destroyed.'

Peter walked up to the post. Looking out across the field, the sycamores had all but disappeared in the gathering dusk, their bare slender tips exposed against the deepening sapphire sky.

'Have I given you body to my own imagination,

Anam?' Peter asked the owl while contemplating the nightfall.

Anam turned and frowned at Peter. 'We knew you were coming, Fireun. It was known long before you arrived here. Though we can never truly live in each other's worlds, we have glimpsed our sacred connection.' Anam swivelled his head and faced the darkening landscape. 'We must wait for Sion. He will be here when the moon appears above the trees.'

Peter sat down, propping his back against the post. Anam was right; some mysterious force had summoned him back to Hope Land. A voice from the wilderness had called him home.

Slowly the rim of the moon edged above the horizon and began its measured climb.

Owl and human sat quietly reposing, watching the moonrise.

A great gust of wind brushed past their faces, carried on over the field. A gussock stirred the tops of the sycamores, followed by a foreboding hush.

'Something's wrong!' cried Anam, craning his head. 'It's Sion. Something's happened!' The wind stirred again, howling now, through the distant trees.

'What do you mean?' asked Peter, jumping to his feet.

Hunching forward, Anam said, 'Fireun, wait here.' He leapt off the post.

'What is it?' yelled Peter. 'What's happened?' But there came no reply—Anam had already disappeared into the darkness.

The telephone rang from the house. Peter hesitated whether to run inside to answer the call or wait for Anam's return. Somewhere across the gloom he heard a long, sad howling. It was not the wind.

'Brigit! Hello!' Peter panted. 'Yes, I was just outside. How are things? My head? Yes, all fine now.' Peter was anxious and could not disguise the matter.

Brigit fed the payphone all her loose change. Something was not right—she felt it. Peter sounded nervous, even afraid. 'Are you sure everything's okay, Peter?' Brigit waved her hand, signalling to Poppy, who stood outside the callbox hailing a taxi. Her friend tapped eagerly on the glass pane of the door, indicating for Brigit to hurry.

'Brigit, there's nothing to worry about,' insisted Peter, catching his breath. He stretched the telephone cord along the hall and peered out the front door. 'Listen, if you must know, I'm waiting to go out with a couple of new friends. Yes, that's right. Their names? Anam and Sion.' He stared out into the dark black night. 'You won't believe me even if I told you.' The words escaped him.

'Try me!' begged Brigit, raising her voice. The cab driver blasted his horn while Poppy ran circles round the phone booth, miming to Brigit to hang up. 'Please, Peter.' She tried to calm herself. 'Who are they?'

Anam's voice rang out, quavering and high-pitched. He appeared from across the field, low and fast, eyes wide, then flew in on a low sweep through the open door. Landing gracelessly on the wooden floor his talons dug deep, leaving scratch marks across the oak boards and, unable to stop sliding, he went crashing into an amphora vase causing it to topple with a mighty crash. Grandfather's ashes lay spilled.

'What's going on, Peter?' yelled Brigit, watching the taxi speed off with Poppy running behind cursing, throwing her hand out with a rude articulated gesture.

Anam emerged from the broken china bearing

the look of deepest dread. 'Fireun! It's Sion! He's caught in a bonebreaker!'

Peter dropped the phone. He picked Anam off the floor, grabbed the torch from the hall and hurried out the door.

Releasing Anam into the air, Peter high-jumped the fence and cut across the field. Anam kept in range above him, like a guardian angel, guiding the way towards Sion's long and frequent howls.

Sion lay writhing in agony by the entrance of his den, his front paw mangled and bloody. The trap had cut deep to the bone. Already he had begun to chew at his leg when Anam arrived.

'Peter is coming! He'll save you,' Anam screeched, landing beside him in a flurry.

Like a beacon of hope, Peter's light shone in the dark, bouncing along as he clambered over the stony hillock up towards Ferne Stone. Peter could clearly hear the awful commotion of the owl's fitful cries coupled with the agonising yowls of the fox.

Kneeling beside Sion, Peter said, 'I'm right here, Sion; you're safe now.' He prised open the metal jaws. The fox collapsed on the earth, weak and feeble, panting, whimpering with pain. Peter reviewed the injured leg. 'Everything will be alright.'

Taking Sion into his arms, he carried him down the hill.

Through drifting clouds, the moon scaled above the hills.

Inside Hope House Sion lay sleeping, stretched out upon the hearthrug by the fire, his wounded leg cleaned and bandaged. Peter dozed next to him in the armchair, clutching a sketchpad in his hand. He had drawn Ferne Stone; engraved the granite top with another of his own Ogham inscriptions:

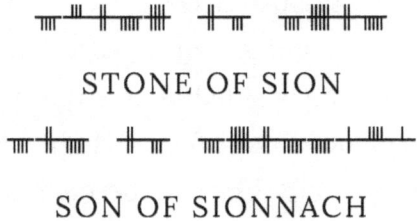

STONE OF SION

SON OF SIONNACH

Outside, the night air snapped cold under freezing fog. The fields were rimed and stiff with frost, glistening like glass under the moonlight. Anam sat resting on the gatepost, weary but grateful Sion was alive. He fluffed himself up into a ball of feathers to keep out the bitter chill. Closed one eye. Then slowly the other.

Anam's sleep was soon interrupted, woken by distant sounds. He heard the scuffling of feet along the north ridge. Looking up, Ghostwood lit up in a strange and eerie glow. Anam widened his gaze, began bobbing and weaving his head, curious as to what it could be.

'What is that?' Anam hooted to himself. He flew over to the house, perched on the windowsill and peered inside. Peter and Sion lay sleeping by the fire. Tapping the window with his beak he began to squawk, scratching at the glass with his sharp claw. Peter stirred, but only to fall deeper into dream. Anam gazed back at the ghostly light, watching it creeping along the ridge, flickering between the trees.

'Only one thing to do.' He sprang off the ledge.

On reaching the ridge, all was dark and quiet. Only the biting wind sounded through the trees, bringing a drizzling of sleet, forcing Anam to draw across the nictitating membrane over his eyes to protect himself from the icy rain. He flew first above the gully surveying the ground below, then, climbing above the treetops, gazed down into Ghostwood.

Suddenly there came the sound of berating crows, their roosting evidently disturbed.

Anam maintained a low-level flight above the trees, flying one direction, then another, looking, scanning the ground for movement. The crows were beginning to settle and in a short space of time, the woods fell silent again. Anam hooted: 'Is everything alright down there?' From the wooded darkness, a spotlight shone directly up into his face, blinding him instantly. Anam could not turn his gaze from the bright glare. He struggled to stay airborne, floundered as the light followed his every move. And then it came. A flash of fire, a loud explosion—lead shot blasting through the treetops.

'Thunderfire!' He let out a long lingering screech. 'Not again!'

With fast-beating wings he banked sharp as another round of shot flew wide, hissing past his face. Blinded by the light, he plunged headlong into the dark awning of trees. Anam did not move or dare make a sound, but sat gripping one of the high branches. The light went out, plunging the woods back into darkness.

He could hear the stealers milling below, tramping through the brushwood. On came the light, shining straight onto the branch where he perched. Caught in the poacher's spotlight, Anam closed his eyes, feared the worst, and waited for the thunder-fire to take him down.

Fenning aimed the gun up at the small, hunched form of the owl, his finger resting on the trigger. 'Gotcha,' he said with a grimace. At once the sky opened in a shower of giant hailstones, stripping leaves and twigs that rained down upon the two men.

'Out of here, Fenning!' yelled Jonas. Shining the spotlight away, Jonas scampered off down the wheeled tracks. Breaking the barrel, Fenning removed the unused cartridge from the gun and made a dash towards the van parked in a small clearing of the wood.

Morgan was slouched over the wheel of the Bedford when Jonas and Fenning returned. The two men threw the guns, the sacks of birds and the spotlight into the back of the van. Morgan lit a half-smoked cigarette and cranked the engine.

Balls of ice the size of walnuts pummelled the van, machine-gunning the windscreen. Morgan yelled, 'Look at the size of those hailstones!' as Jonas and Fenning scrambled into the van.

Jonas snatched Morgan's cigarette from his mouth and took a long drag. 'Almost bagged us an owl.' He scowled out the window at the rain of ice-bullets. 'Bloody weather! Still, we did get lucky with the snare this time.'

In a few minutes, a ceasefire. Hail turned to sleet as the vehicle pulled away, slipping in the muddy tracks, causing a wire cage in the back of the van to slide and bang against the side.

Sheltered under a covering of pine cones, Anam watched the glow of the van move away. Promptly, he decided to follow. He hurried into the air and through the woods he sped, flitting from tree to tree, keeping a favourable distance, now and then having need to perch and shake off the freezing rain from his soaked and tousled feathers.

As the van emerged from the forest, the stealers attempted to follow the tracks along the edge of the gully heading towards the rise. Anam flew close behind, watching as the van slid wildly, causing the cage in the back to slam up against the tailgate. With engine backfiring, gears grinding, the Bedford came to a slippery standstill close to the edge of the gully. A rear wheel sunk into the sod, spinning freely, digging itself deeper into the rut. Anam circled back on himself, alighting on a high branch at the edge of the forest. He could hear the stealers cursing the weather as they climbed out of the van. Fenning began ramming bits of dead wood under the bogged wheel and while Morgan revved the engine, Jonas pushed against the back of the Bedford, mud spattering his face.

Anam flew to a lower branch. He could see down into the rear of the pickup. A sack had split open, spilling out a heap of dead birds. Among the carnage was the body of a badger, its banded face staring vacantly up at him. Anam noticed the telltale shot hole through the animal's ear. *Poor Brogan.* Anam heard a shuffling of feet from inside the wire cage. Elan Hare hobbled to the door, his front foot hanging limp, wounded by a snare wire. Behind the hare, some other smaller creature sat huddled in the corner of the cage.

The engine screamed while the wheel spun uselessly, axle-deep in mud. The heavy rains brought a deluge of water, flooding the tracks, eroding the rim and coursing over the gully. With heads bent, Jonas and Fenning heaved and groaned, pushing pitifully against the dead weight of the vehicle, but to no gain—they could not stop the Bedford from edging towards the precipice.

Anam gave a gentle call, *Kiew*, hoping the stealers would not hear him over their own racket. He dropped silently from the tree, landing quietly on top of the cage. Elan sat paralysed with fear. Anam called to him, *Kiew! Kiew!*—'Elan! Elan!' His calling made the other animal trembling in the back of the cage look up at him.

'Cara!' cried Anam. 'Cara, is that you?'

The terrified squirrel shuffled across the cage floor, her hind leg bleeding from a pellet shot that penetrated the flesh. She gazed through the wire mesh. 'Oh, Anam, I'm so sorry,' she whimpered, stricken with sorrow, 'we never stood a chance.'

Anam had never seen such anguish and despair as he did in Cara's face. He swivelled his head sharp, seeing the stealers slipping and sliding in the mire, hearing their cursing, their shouting at one another. The gleam in Anam's eyes spoke his rage and his heart beat fast. The nubilous membrane slid across his eyes as he prepared for battle. Then off he flew, upwards and upwards, the hard rain lashing his face. Higher and higher he climbed until he disappeared above the woods.

Strong winds blew across the ridge, boughs bending, breaking in the gale force. With wings tucked at his side, Anam made one gallant charge and dived down towards the ground. Levelling to a swoop—*Kee-ik!*—the owl struck the back of Fenning's neck, his razor claws dug deep into muscle. Fenning's legs buckled as he collapsed facedown into the mud. Jonas looked up to see the owl's terrifying talons heading straight for him and with no time to turn or fend, the outspread claws ripped across his face.

Inside the van, Morgan stared out at Fenning flailing his arms to evade the crazy raptor. A blood-soaked hand smacked hard against the side of the van—Morgan turned—Jonas appeared at the window, terror-stricken, trying desperately to open the door. Anam swooped. A direct hit to the head sent Jonas screaming.

Morgan was all alone. He rammed the gears and pushed the accelerator. Down the gully the vehicle plunged. Morgan gripped the steering wheel but mastered no control over the van as it careered down the ravine, ripping through shrubs, bouncing over rocks and tossing out the cage. Side-swiping a fir tree clinging halfway up the bank, the van flipped onto its roof before striking hard against a protruding boulder. With one mighty scream, the engine throttled up and died. Gradually the wheels stopped turning.

Kicking out the windscreen, Morgan clambered through the broken glass and went running for his life. The cage lay on the ground, its door ruptured open.

Anam flew down the gorge, calling wildly, *Kiew, kiew, kiew!* 'Run, Elan, run!' The hare hobbled out from the cage, went limping off down the hillside.

Anam poked his head through the broken wire door.

'It's okay, Cara. I'm right here.'

Cara crawled cautiously up to the metal flap, her ears pressed back, eyes wide with fear as she looked out at Anam. 'You're safe now, Cara,' said Anam. 'Everything will be alright.'

Second Gathering

Sion stood on Ferne Stone, leg bandaged, eyes fixed upon the crowd.

Many more animals throughout the land, from field and vale, attended the gathering. The chatter of a thousand creatures lulled to a calm when Sion raised his paw. He looked over the multitude before him. Predator and prey united, each standing close to the other.

On the stone platform next to Sion sat Anam, his eyes widening with delight—high in the branches of the ash tree he could see Otus deep in conversation with a baby merlin, teaching the bird the ways of the wing and the secret to silent flight. Anam bounced with joy when Otus turned to him, nodded and winked.

'To rid the land of stealers,' said Sion, 'we must first learn to live peacefully among ourselves. The time has come for change, for us to gather, embrace our diversities, and live communally as friend and neighbour.'

Faces turned to one another; kestrel and king-fisher; stoat and dormouse; weasel and rabbit. They all began talking in the language of ancient earth, each asking the same question—'How can we *all* be friends?'

Anam took a long, deep breath. 'We will have to alter our eating habits.' The animals stood, solemn-faced. Anam gave it to them straight. 'We must learn not to prey on one another. We must change to a diet of plants, berries and herbs. Any meat eaters will have to turn herbivore.' The raptors and weasels looked troubled; hunting was in their blood and Anam knew of the difficulties they would face to curb their killer instinct. 'For some of you, it will take a bit of getting used to; perhaps keep to a few fish, bugs and beetles, just to help with the adjustment.' Anam leaned back, fluffed his feathers and let out an endearing hoot. 'I know we can do this,' he said in earnest.

Bleating loudly, Keyrrey Ewe and Eayn Lamb picked their way across the flint-strewn earth, climbed the table of stone and ambled up to Sion. The crowd ceased their ambivalent chatter and stood quietly in awe. When Sion placed his bandaged paw upon the head of the lamb, a great gasp of astonishment issued from every animal.

'An age of corruption reigns upon us,' proclaimed Sion. 'Brutality and tyranny have darkened our land. We end this cruel curse by building ourselves a community. Codes of conduct are formed in every society—codes which are radically alike among all species. Equality, compatibility and cooperation is a life in harmony with nature. We all know on raising a family our first instinct is to nurture and protect. We just need to extend our caring nature to include all living creatures.' Sion had their full attention. 'By bringing together our differences we will see how similar we really are. Combining our strengths and talents is how we will survive, and embracing love according to the needs and values of the tribe is how we shall conquer our fear of man.'

The multitude of hopeful faces looked on with growing eagerness. Now they wanted answers—they needed a resolution to the troubles of their world.

Sion continued: 'To make this all possible, a mediator is required; one who walks between two realms—animal and human alike.' The creatures seemed less troubled than before on hearing Sion's proclamation, more accepting of the prediction that a human shall enter their world. 'Today, a prophecy has been fulfilled. Our mediator has appeared: his name is Fireun, and he stands here among us.'

Kiew, kiew! Anam gave the signal. Peter came out from under the stone table carrying Cara in his hands. Primal instinct sent every creature fleeing for its life.

WUH! WUH! 'WAIT! WAIT!' barked Sion.

The animals stopped in their tracks and looked back. Sion maintained his stance. 'It is foretold that one man be chosen to join us. This is Fireun, the chosen one. We must entrust in him our future, for the fate of Hope Land lies solely in his hands.'

In the air of silence that followed, every confused and frightened animal glanced warily at each other, then at Fireun, realising the time for change had come. Each neighbour wittingly surrendered their differences. Calmly and genially, one by one, they showed leniency towards the other.

'We must abandon the belief we are of a divided kingdom,' counselled Sion. 'Though we are many and varied, we coexist in one world, we are all connected, inseparable. Join us, comrades, and help preserve the future. Help bring peace back to the tribes of Hope Land.'

Fireun stepped up onto the stone lintel, placed Cara down between Anam and Sion and raised both hands in the air. 'To those wreaking havoc upon the land, the tide must turn,' said Fireun. 'Their own wave of violence shall strike back against them. Eye for an eye.' The animals moved closer, sat quietly and listened. 'We humans have an ancient adage, a most modest code for living—*treat your neighbour as you would like to be treated.*'

A shaft of sunlight broke through the clouds, shone down on Fireun, his hair bronzed with a deep radiance. The animals felt they could trust this human; he was special, he was one of them, and they flocked closer together. Compelled by curiosity, ushered by necessity, every creature congregated around the stone altar.

'We may appear dissimilar,' continued Fireun, 'we look different, sound different, but beneath our appearances, we are each born of this earth, each warmed by the same sun.' The animals huddled, shoulder to shoulder, wing to wing. 'Every tree, every rock, every river, bird and beast—all are indissolubly joined.'

Anam flew onto Peter's shoulder. 'Humans are more like us than we realise,' Anam hooted. 'Their basic needs are the same. Water, food and shelter are their foundations for living. They have the same fears and suffer as we do. They differ only by seeking pleasure in pain and taking more than their fair needs.'

'Greed has become their god,' squeaked Cara, scrambling up onto Peter's other shoulder, flanking Anam. 'Greed is the real enemy!' Her red tail quivered. 'Greed provokes fighting and killing, even among their kind.'

Sion raised his paw. 'Divided we stand vulnerable; gathered and we are a rock of strength and stability. Unity is the only way we overcome our opponents.'

There was a moment of quiet reflection. Then the air thickened. A cloud of uncertainty drifted over the animals. How could they oppose the stealers? What power or cunning had they? They were humble creatures, without the skill of coercion, and knew not the ways of trickery. Not a whisker twitched nor feather ruffled. Looking up at Fireun standing on the rock, each bewildered creature began to realise hope was all they had. Perhaps this human *was* the only way. Perhaps he could help write the next chapter of their lives?

Bryony Badger was the first to step forward, ushering her pups, prompting Merlyn Blackbird and Brych Thrush to take leave from the alder, landing next to Sion. Next came Rudhek Robin and Dreean Wren, flittering down from the aspen. Connyn Rabbit, although hesitant at first, hopped closer with his kits. Hazel Dormouse came darting out from beneath a rock, weaving through the spread feet of a weasel, who snarled and spat as she passed.

Every animal seemed to inspire the other. Kasek Woodpecker and Cruidín Kingfisher flew from the hawthorn and perched on the lintel, facing the crowd. High up in the ash, the raptors watched the bond of friendship forming, realising they too were family and part of a greater clan. Dobran Otter and Greynog Hedgehog traversed the rocky ground together, both choosing to be in on the act. With each step closer to Ferne Stone, the animals felt the burden of doubt lift away, their fears bridled with hope.

But Bronwen Weasel and Nathair Snake did not; their minds were closed and unable to make the leap beyond their natural instincts.

'You're all fools,' mocked the snake, raising her venomous head and vulgarly exposing her fangs. 'It's every creature for itself.'

'You can't change what you already are,' wrangled the weasel. 'It's survival of the fittest. Kill or be killed.'

Nathair Snake lunged at the heel of Bronwen Weasel, causing her to jump with a sideways hop, spitting and snarling. The two creatures made off in opposite directions—weasel bounded into the broom; snake slithered beneath the long grass.

The sun shone its evening light upon the lingerers. There was a growing comradeship shared between bird and beast. Where once stood archenemies, new friendships had formed.

Sion looked to Fireun, Cara glanced at Anam, each sharing a pleasing exchange of gestures, for all the animals had completely encircled the stone. Being alive no longer seemed dangerous or frightening to them. They were a united kingdom and each carried a seed of hope in their heart.

'We are gathered, and we are one,' said Peter, and with Cara sitting comfortably on one shoulder, Anam on the other, he took Sion into his arms and carried him home.

A Small Act of Love

'm worried about Peter,' said Brigit, letting out a woeful sigh. Still in make-up, wearing the face of a horse, she slumped down on a wooden crate bathed in the blue light of the gantry. Bearing goat head and horns, Poppy trudged across the stage to sit beside her on a straw bale. The collapsed windmill stood in shadow behind them. In front, two thousand vacant seats stretched out in tiered rows.

Shoulders hunched, Brigit cast her eyes to the floor in a pensive stare. She appeared tired and troubled. 'He isn't the same man I knew when he lived in the city,' she mourned. 'He's living in a world of his own, seems so … far away, so … *elsewhere.*' She looked up at her friend. 'He's lost touch with reality.'

'What makes you say that?' asked Poppy, studying her lines from the play script.

'He says strange things … like … animals *talk* to him! That *he* can *talk* to them!' Brigit threw her arms up in exasperation, quickly dropping them again into her lap. 'He's out with the owls, running with the foxes, all hours of the night and day!' She swung her heavy horse head at Poppy. 'He's disappeared into another world!'

Poppy looked up from reading her scene and gawked at Brigit.

'He's a writer,' replied Poppy. 'An artist becomes part of their art. It's called imagination! We're no different, Brigit.' She held up the script. 'Look here— you're acting a horse and I'm an old goat!' Brigit laughed when Poppy jiggled her eyebrows, chewing on a piece of straw in jest. 'We're all living in other worlds, sweetie.' She smiled.

Back in reflection, Brigit sat pondering the situation, mulling things over in her mind, wondering what she could do. Snapping out of her thoughts, she proclaimed, 'I have to go back and see him. I should be there for him. His world is my world, whatever and wherever that may be.' Her doleful eyes suddenly lit up. 'I'll drive to Nemeton tonight!'

'*Tonight?*' bleated Poppy, her voice filling the theatre. She threw down the script, appalled at the idea. 'You can't just up and run. What about the play? We have full dress rehearsals tomorrow. We open in a week. You're under contract!' Poppy leaned closer and took hold of Brigit's hands, squeezing her fingers gently, eyes pleading. 'You belong here, on the stage. The theatre is your world.'

Dropping her shoulders, Brigit yielded to her friend's advice. 'You're right, Popps ... the show must go on.' She forced a deep breath, letting out a soft snort and embraced Poppy's hands. 'I miss him terribly.' She held a longing look, shedding a solitary tear that rolled down her muzzle. 'I love him, I really do—deeply, madly, irrevocably.'

The two thespians gazed at each other for a quiet moment before the gantry light switched off, plunging the stage into darkness.

Silence of The Fields

Not a crow, not a rook, not a raven, wheeled above the north ridge.

The church stood silent on the hill.

Along the narrow coomb the sky was heavy with thick white clouds, reaching down to the valley. A lingering mist veiled the old, abandoned farmhouse.

In the scullery, upon the workbench, stood a wireframe of a fox, part-covered with papier-mâché, sculptured into muscle and sinew, carving out the shape of limb and torso—an unfinished project awaiting its hide.

Balorid sat watching Dearg taking great pleasure in skinning a cat—sickening as it was even to him.

Dearg ran a scalpel along the underbelly from throat to tail; such precision would minimise the seam when the animal was later reassembled.

'We can't do much of this home-grown stuff,' grumbled Balorid, inhaling on a cigarette before flicking it at Dearg—the butt bounced off his shoulder in a micro-explosion of tiny orange sparks and landed smouldering on the floor. 'Word would soon spread round this sleepy old town that dear little pets were disappearing.'

Balorid brooded and rolled another cigarette.

Dearg cut round the nape and skull of the cat, separating the facial skin from meat and bone using tiny incisions of the scalpel. 'Traps have been empty for days,' Dearg remarked, wiping his hands down his apron. 'There's nothing else for me to work with. Go for a walk, see for yourself. The woods are bare, fields are empty. Not a dumb critter anywhere to be found.'

'Well, do something about it!' demanded Balorid, thumping the bench and upsetting a tray of glass eyes that went rolling over the table like marbles. 'This is bad for business.'

'We'll have to travel farther out with traps and

guns,' Dearg replied, placing the glass beads, one by one, back inside the container, pausing to compare each shape and colour.

'An entire population of birds and animals don't just vanish!' thundered Balorid, his wrinkly eyelid jittering.

The cat's coat, once removed, was washed in a tub of water, then left to soak in a bath of acetone. 'I blame those bumbling boneheads,' said Dearg. 'They couldn't catch a worm to fish with.'

Balorid let out a long, frustrated grunt. 'Where are those bloody morons anyway? They haven't shown up for days. Let's go track them down.'

Dearg picked up the smouldering cigarette lying by his foot, puffing it back to life, letting the smoke linger between his lips. He selected a glass bead and held it to the light. 'Eye for an eye,' he remarked.

It was true, the woods and fields lay empty and silent. Trees were vacant of birdsong. Not even the usual buzz of bee nor chirp of cricket along the hedgerows.

Outside Beith Barn, Balorid pointed the shotgun into the air and pulled the trigger. Not a creature stirred, not even a mouse. The loud boom rumbled and died. Again, he fired the gun and screamed a blasphemy to the sky. Reloading, he emptied another two rounds. The shots echoed and faded.

At Ferne Stone, Dearg dug his heel idly among the loose pebbles. Balorid checked the trap, seeing it had been fired, noticing dry blood on the stone. But no fox.

'Bah!' Balorid pulled the anchor chain out of the ground and slung the trap over his shoulder.

Ghostwood was the same; eerily silent, empty of life.

Crammed inside a small Morris car, Balorid and Dearg stared out the dirt-smeared windscreen, both looking flummoxed and lost for words. They drove from the woods, following the deep muddy tracks along the ridge, their heads jostling as the car dipped in and out of watery potholes. They made their way back towards the rise. Neither noticed that in the gully below lay the Bedford van, upturned against a granite rock.

It was at the junction by the drystone wall that Nathair Snake came side-winding across the lane in search of a meal in the adjoining field. There came two dampened thuds as Balorid steered the car over her sleek muscular body.

'Nobody likes snakes,' he grimaced.

A FanTabulous Ruse

Saille Lake was a haven for otters. Hedgehogs waddled through the sedge grass. Rabbits and badgers made their warrens along the sandy banks. Squirrels built their drays high up in the forks of tall trees. In the elder, woodpeckers lived in peaceful society with cuckoos. Blackbirds sang from the slender birch, accompanied by song thrushes and nightingales. Robins and wrens took up residence in the aspen and juniper. Ospreys, hawks and kestrels nested aloft the ash, where neighbouring rooks, ravens and crows roosted in the crown of a magnificent beech. The hollowed trunk of a rowan provided home for families of field mice, voles and shrews. *Earth Angels*. It was Peter's finest painting, detailing companionship, capturing the true spirit of unity and love.

One cold wintry night, when frost laced the window, Sion sat inside Hope House warming his haunches by the fire, mesmerised by the flickering flames. Anam and Cara sat together on Peter's shoulder watching Peter sketching a cluster of hazelnuts.

'We haven't won yet, Sion,' said Peter, looking up from his scribal desk. 'We may be safe on Hope Land, but stealers can be replaced. New ones will come.' He dipped the quill and scratched ink across the paper. 'What Anam has done—he has plucked the bad seeds from the earth. Now we must find a way to pull out the roots.' Peter continued shading Coll Spring and the ring of hazel trees.

Sion turned and spoke to Peter: 'We are here to help you conceive such a plan, Fireun. Show us what we must do to rid us of the stealers, so we may fulfil the prophecy of peace and bring freedom back to our land.'

Peter nodded to Sion, removed the drawing and held it out for him to see—a medley of pen and ink sketches of all his friends. Anam was drawn perched on the gatepost, the shadow of Ghostwood looming behind. Sion he presented standing proud upon his stone house, silhouetted against the setting sun. Cara hugged the trunk of a hazel bush, her eyes wide and full of youthful zeal.

Peter placed the paper on the desk to dry and, fastening a fresh sheet on the easel, dipped and poised his pen once more, ready to begin another drawing. He gazed over at Dobran Otter sprawled out on the sofa. He noticed Brân Raven perched on the bookcase. On the stroke of one, Lugh Wood Mouse came running down the longcase clock, jumping up onto the armchair to sit with Sion by the fire.

'Here's what we do,' said Peter to his band of merry helpers. Beginning with rudimentary outlines he sketched the tumbledown farmhouse, part-hidden along a pathway choked with blackthorn and nettle. He added in the huge round chimney, overgrown with tendrils of ivy. Some darker shade to the sky brought sallow, stormy clouds rolling in over the coomb. With crosshatching and with stippling, making patterns from dots and dashes, he rendered light and shade, bringing solidity, tone and texture to the stealers' hideaway.

Slipping the paper out from under its clip, Peter inserted a fresh sheet and moved on to the next part of the montage. From quick inky lines there soon appeared the body of an owl, wings tucked to its side, diving in a vertical stoop between the pine trees. From Peter's shoulder, Anam rocked side-to-side, bounced with amusement at seeing a true-life image of himself appear on paper.

The spontaneity and fluidity of each stroke were as much part of Peter's personality as the subjects he drew. He made play of the pen with long sweeping lines, confident flicks and little intricate marks that gave form and depth. Once the drawing was complete, so he began another.

The animals gathered on the desk with Lugh Wood Mouse now sitting on the carriage of the typewriter. All waited with anticipation for the next scene.

Ink flowed freely through the night, into the early hours of a new morning. The smallfolk huddled and gabbled, helping Peter draw up their plan of action. More lines, more squiggles, dots and dashes, and there appeared three pairs of eyes of varying shape and size, of mustelid, murid and sciuridae.

This drawing depicted an otter, a mouse and a squirrel lying in wait inside a wooden crate, above which stood a dark, hooded figure, holding out a lantern. Applying various pressures to the nib, Peter fashioned the play of light and shadow, casting an eerie atmosphere to the picture. In the background, he sketched in a large black raven with a dagger-like beak, peering in through a broken windowpane. The animals marvelled over the final details of the finished scene.

By dawn, the embers had turned to fine-powdered ash. The hearthstone lay cold and grey against the morning. The chairs and sofa stood empty facing the fireplace.

Peter was alone working hard at his easel, a paintbrush in each hand, another pressed between his lips. The desk was strewn with pens and paints, and the walls were adorned with illustrations of Sion, Anam, Cara and many of the animals he had come to know.

All day he worked the canvas, painting the landscape seen from his window. With careful brush-strokes, he left tiny daubs of brilliant white—as of gleams of light reflecting on the lake. On the eastern

212

rise, he painted the church, its grey bell tower pointing to the sky and borne in with the sound of its chimes, added a single bead of iridescent copper paint to the weathercock that crowned the spire. Swapping brushes, he dabbed deep accents of indigo to the sycamores on the horizon. And in radiant shadow he coloured the north ridge and the ghostly wood, rendering a strong level of contrast to the tops of trees that created a sudden falloff into darkness.

Stepping back from the canvas, there came an afterthought—from flecks of brown, dabs of white and tan, he added in his own visionary touch: two spread eagles, soaring high over the hills, completed the scene.

Peter was pleased at having captured the charm of his native vale.

Without pause to rest, clearing space, he sat at the typewriter and flexed his fingers.

EarTh Angels

The sun glittered gold across the water.

Fireun walked with Sion along the lakeside, calling the animals together, inviting one and all to join them under the willow tree. Creatures of every kind followed in procession down along the shoreline, with Keyrrey Ewe and Eayn Lamb leading the tribe. Next came Bryony Badger ushering her pups. Connyn Rabbit and his kits went splashing in the shallows, chasing after Dobran Otter, while Greynog Hedgehog trundled behind as fast as her little legs would carry her—and not once did she have the need to roll into her impenetrable ball.

With great excitement, Elan Hare started snorting and thumping the ground with his hind foot, cheering out for Lugh Wood Mouse, who, having climbed high into the branches of the tallest beech, ranked alongside Brân Raven, standing to attention and ready for action.

Anam and Otus flew abreast across the lake, their friendship reunited in common cause. Otus flew up inside the willow tree while Anam perched on Fireun's shoulder, shaded under the draping branches. The band of animals grouped together, all communing in the ancient language. It was an atmosphere of great expectation and simmering excitement.

Feòrag Squirrel gently rubbed noses with Cara, offering her a nuptial hazelnut, holding it aptly between his forepaws. She looked adoringly at the golden-brown kernel. Flashing her eyes and with flirting tail, she stuffed the nut inside the pocket of her cheek and went skipping across the ground, springing up Fireun's leg, sitting next to Anam.

Birds of all variety perched in every tree. A dragonfly came darting over the water to land on a bulrush, her tail in elegant repose, while Losgann Frog broke out his evening chant.

Fireun looked upon his band of brave and true-hearted companions.

'Tonight, we end all fear,' he announced. 'Blight and bane will be blotted out.' A loud acclamation erupted from the animals, filling the air with their screeches and squawks, bleats and squeaks, hoots and snorts—a merriment of a hundred creatures.

'On this coming moonless night,' continued Fireun, 'one stealer shall be alone in Ghostwood, the other in the old abandoned house. Their time of reckoning is upon them.' Each animal reached out their paw and wing to touch the hand of Fireun.

'We are resolute and we are strong,' he said to them. 'Are you ready to defeat the stealers?' Once more the air filled with the uproar of mirth and revelry.

'Good luck, Anam,' yipped Sion over the noisy banter.

'Providence be with you, Sion, my dear friend,' hooted Anam.

With the sun resting on the western hills, Fireun sat with his earth angels.

'I have entered your world, as you have mine,' he said. 'Tomorrow will dawn the beginning of a new time. It will be written—in the final hour of struggle, we shall strive, and we will triumph!'

The Battle of Balorid

Deep in the night, Dearg came stomping through Ghostwood, crushing the bracken stalks underfoot. He stopped beside a tree stump and adjusted a small torchlight strapped to his head. Slinging his gun across his back, he picked up a dead branch from the ground and began poking around the base of the stump. In an instant, the jaws of a trap sprung out of the earth, its steel teeth snapping the deadwood. Dearg stood wincing, scratching his head, perplexed as to why no animal had already fired the trap. He bent down to examine the triggering mechanism under the light. Prising the jaws open with the heel of his boot, he reset the spring and repositioned the plate. Checking that the anchor chain was firmly fastened, and the rod driven securely into the ground, he used the remainder of the branch to sweep the earth level, carefully concealing the pan and jaws under a cover of leaves.

Using the stick, he gouged a hole into the ground a few inches out from the stump. Keeping his hands free from touching the earth, as to not leave any trace of human scent, he made the hole appear as if a small animal had recently burrowed and was nesting there. Stuffing a piece of rabbit meat inside the hole, he took a small glass bottle from his breast pocket and dribbled a few drops of animal lure directly onto the stump. Gloating, Dearg stepped back and admired his work. 'There'll be no weaselling out of this one,' he said.

Independently, the trees began to lean, lunging like living things. A squall roared through the pines, making them moan and groan as their tops started whipping back and forth.

Anam descended at great speed, diving in a stoop between the buffeting branches. With wings tucked, he maintained his downward dive to the ground and at the last moment, levelling out, went sweeping low over the ground towards the stealer.

Sensing something swoop past his head, Dearg looked up just as Anam disappeared into shadow. Dearg gazed about him, his light illuminating the columns of trees, their high tops thrashing about. Seeing nothing, hearing nothing, other than the roaring wind, he crouched down to spread the leaves and cover his tracks.

Above the treetops, high up into the stormy sky, Anam climbed to a stall. With nictitating membranes sliding into position, wings folded, he went diving back to earth, feeling the sting of the aigrish wind against his face.

This time Dearg felt the brush of a wing pass his cheek. He stood and whipped around, seeing Anam speed off into the woods. Dearg held out the dead-wood like a cudgel, ready to strike. From behind, Anam came swooping between the tree trunks, sent a claw combing through the stealer's hair and, with a tight curve, around he came, preparing for another airstrike. Dearg lunged out at the owl, but Anam was too quick, too nimble; he rolled and yawed, then rose and dived again. Dearg spun on his heels, lashing out with another futile swing.

On each pass, Dearg became more and more vexed at his failures to smite the owl. Anam wasn't finished. He toyed with the stealer, coming from one side, then another. *Kiew!* he cried, for stealing Brogan. *Kiew-Kiew!* for poor Connie and her kittens. Advancing straight towards the stealer—*Kiew-Kiew-Kiew!* for every animal stolen from wood and field. Raging, Dearg charged and swung the branch, missing Anam but striking out against a tree. In a splintering of wood fragments, the tip of the branch fractured off, rebounding, hitting Dearg square across the brow. Anam turned sharp, came straight back for a final attack, beak open, talons out. Dearg threw the remaining wood, which struck Anam, dashing the little owl to the ground. Tumbling over and over, Anam hit hard against the tree stump. Already Dearg was looming over him, face streaked with blood. Powerless, Anam watched with horror as the stealer pointed a thunderfire to his head.

'You're a dead rat!'

'STOP! STOP! STOP!' cried Peter.

The drapes billowed into the room. A whorl of leaves came blasting through the window, sending scores of typed pages into the air.

Peter stared at the typewriter, at the page he was working on, reading aloud his printed words— 'You're a dead rat!' He rose from his seat and hurried to the window, pulling open the drapes. For a moment it was Anam's face reflected in the wet glass. 'It's okay, Little Owl. I'm right here.' Closing the window, latching it firmly, he watched the fury of rain and leaves lash against the pane. Turning, mulling over the pictures pinned on the wall, Peter studied the pen-and-ink drawing of Anam charging in a steep dive between the pine trees. Pondering the scene for a while, he dipped his quill into the inkwell and made a slight alteration to the picture. With a few short strokes, some squiggles and crosshatching, he drew in the figure of a long-eared owl, sitting high on a branch watching over Anam.

Returning to the window, Peter looked out at the wild night; the wind blowing a storm, leaves tossing about in the air. 'Everything will be alright.' He closed the drapes.

Peter sat back at the desk, fingers hammering away on the typewriter.

Trees groaned in a williwar of protest, fuelled by the howling winds. Rains pummelled the earth.

Dearg stood towering over Anam, gun in hand, ready to shoot. 'You're stuffed!' he said, thumbing back the hammer, a merciless grin widening across his bloodied face.

Scalpel-sharp claws ripped a tussock of hair clean from Dearg's scalp. Bawling like a hog, he swung violently on his heel. Otus flew high, ghosting into the treetops. Dearg turned to finish Anam—but he was gone. Otus struck again, this time the neck, eight talons tearing the flesh. Stumbling to the ground, dropping the gun, Dearg reached out with open hands to break his fall. The trap fired—steel teeth snapped, tearing through his jacket sleeve, biting deep into his forearm.

The stealer's cold-curdling scream resounded through the woods; his ghastly wails echoed out across the ridge and far along the rise.

Otus and Anam landed jointly on the tree stump, calmly observing the stealer caught by his own bonebreaker.

U-eek! Otus screeched.

Kee-ik! screeched Anam.

Balorid looked sharp to the sound of distant screams. Was it the cry of the banshee? Or perhaps just the howling of the wind along the path, gathering up hoary clouds over the coomb. Balorid battled against the gale—a mighty force that stayed his progress and tossed off his hat. He brushed past the blackthorn that shook with fury, its savage branches clattering like teeth, clapperclawing his coat and ripping the cloth. 'Bah!' he cursed.

Hastening into the house, slamming the door behind, Balorid struck a match and lit the paraffin lamp. He checked his watch. 'You're late, Dearg,' he griped. The wind whistled mournfully through the broken windowpanes. The lantern swung from side to side and with head bent, shoulders hunched, he moved his shadow through the house.

In the scullery, Balorid wheeled the trolley bearing an animal mount. Lit by the lamplight, Bronwen Weasel stood suspended in time, mouth frozen in the act of consuming a shrew, her sharp teeth penetrating the neck behind the vermin's ear. Balorid pushed the trolley across the floor to a stack of crates, where he placed the stuffed creature inside an open box and covered it over with a layer of packing-straw. With a few blows of a crowbar, Balorid nailed the lid down.

He checked the time again. 'Bah! Nearly midnight! Where in damnation?' Taking a cigarette from his pocket, he was about to light up when a sound from behind made him pause and slowly turn his head. There it was again, a definite scuffling—of something scratching over the flagstone floor. Straining to listen, he held up the lantern. A moment passed and he heard nothing more. Upon striking the match the sound returned. Louder this time, a definite scurrying of feet, of tiny claws scampering over the stone. Balorid held out the lamp, looking about the shadowy room. There was nothing but the wind whipping the tattered curtains. Puffing on the cigarette pressed firmly between his lips, he pushed the trolley against the wall. Again, a scuffling of feet, this time followed by the clinking of glass. He swung out the lamp. 'Who's there!' he bellowed. There came a loud breaking smash. 'Is that you, Dearg?' But no one answered.

Creeping across the floor, past the table and chairs, Balorid studied the metal rack, peering between rows of jars: methanol, borax and a beaker of glass eyes. He felt a crunching of something fracturing under his boot. A broken decanter lay on the floor, its liquid freshly spilled.

Above him on the top shelf, a small rodent whipped behind a bottle of formaldehyde, causing it to wobble on its base. As Balorid watched the bottle come to a rest, a quick scurrying of feet behind sent him spinning around, his beady eye catching sight of the mouse before it scampered into shadow.

Sourly he searched the room, lumbering along the line of crates, inspecting each one, holding up the lantern to peer inside. A quick flick of a tail slipped beneath the packing-straw. Across the room came a loud tapping at the window. The grating of claws on glass sent Balorid spinning on his heels. 'Who's there!?' Bent and rigid, Balorid stood staring at the window, at the torn curtains flapping like gigantic gargoyle wings.

Lugh Wood Mouse slipped out from the crate and ran across the floor. He stopped, looked fearlessly up at Balorid towering above him. Standing on his hind legs, Lugh lifted his whiskered pink nose high in the air and squeaked boldly. Balorid glared down at the tiny creature. Away the mouse streaked. It dashed back up the side of the wooden crate and burrowed into the straw.

Balorid picked up the crowbar, held ready to strike, and crept towards the crate.

Lugh peeped his head out, gave another belligerent squeak and slipped back under the loose packing. With crowbar poised in one hand, Balorid lifted the lantern with his other and moved closer to the crate. Stooping to look inside, there came a dreadful shriek. Needle-sharp teeth lunged as Dobran Otter leapt out, fixing his bone-crushing molars into Balorid's nose. Screaming like a hare, Balorid stumbled backwards; the iron slipped from his hand and struck the stone floor with a resounding clang. The lantern dropped and smashed in a pool of burning oil.

Brân Raven flew in through the broken window, squawking, 'Nevermore! Nevermore! Nevermore!' and with wild flapping wings, hustled Balorid hard against the rack of chemicals. Jars of arsenic and caustic crystals came crashing down, smashing over his head. A beaker toppled, sending hundreds of glass eyes spilling across the floor. Balorid made to escape, slipped, fell backwards to the ground. With head badly gashed and bleeding, face covered with corrosive powders, he looked up at the one remaining bottle on the rack that toppled and was rolling along the top shelf.

Out of the crate jumped Cara, who went scampering across the stone floor, leaping onto Balorid's chest, squealing in his face with all her mighty wrath. The eye of death sprang open. But Cara was not afraid—she stared right back, screeching, chastising him for all he stood for.

Balorid looked up to the tinkling of glass. The bottle of formaldehyde rolled to a precarious standstill with its spout overhanging the shelf right above him. Thrusting out his hand, Balorid fumbled for the crowbar. But Brân Raven jabbed at his knuckles with his stout pointed beak. *Cr-r-ruck!* 'Nevermore!'

Scurrying up the rack, Lugh raced across the shelf and began to chew at the cork of the projecting jar. Balorid looked on, powerless, horrified as formaldehyde began to seep through the stopper. Cara leapt to the floor as Lugh continued to gnaw. With one mighty lunge of his incisors, the seal broke, pouring the noxious solution down onto Balorid's face. How he bayed like a wild animal, pained and full of fury. The room filled with a cacophony of squawks and squeaks mixed with Balorid's own defeated cries.

Dobran, Cara, Brân and Lugh fled out the window, leaving Balorid alone in the house. The burning puddle of oil spread across the floor, igniting bales of packing-straw and causing crates to burst into flame. Blinded, Balorid struggled to get away. With slow and feeble motions he dragged himself across the floor, bellying like a snake.

The house was ablaze when Balorid crawled out. Low clouds hugged the hills and rolled down the narrow coomb. In howling gales he grovelled along the path, stumbling blindly into a thicket of black-thorn. In the deathly tangle of briar, his sightless sockets stared out between the barbed branches. Blood trickled down his white-powdered cheeks. The more he struggled, the deeper the thorns pierced his flesh. Resigning, Balorid gave one long lingering breath, 'Baah ...!' before his mouth stiffened and his body lay still.

The wind quickly calmed and ceased its bitter fury. Soon the only sound was the burning building, its crippled roof collapsing in a thunder of fire, shooting streams of sparks high into the air.

Far away the village bell rang the midnight hour and as the last chime faded, faint sprinkles of snow began to fall; a scattering of white flakes swirling above the burning roof, instantly melting in the bellowing flames. But the clouds rolled and the snow thickened. A blizzard blew, white-washing the landscape, and gradually the flames ceased their roar.

By dawn, the remains of the roof had been completely covered by heavy snowfall and the house stood silent in the vale. The jungle of nettle and blackthorn lay buried beneath a soft white mantle. Out among cottage and church and down the valley the snow had drifted, wrapping the woods and fields under the rime of winter.

Back To Earth

The gentle green giant graced the shore, her acuminate tips gently stroking the water.

With rapid wingbeats and looping glides, Anam Little Owl came streaking across the lake, sweeping straight up to a small cavity in the willow's trunk, perching there momentarily before vanishing inside.

Anam rubbed beaks with Athene Little Owl, presenting her with a small stem of flowers picked fresh from the elder. She whooped soft affections, carefully turning a clutch of white eggs that lay beneath her breast. Anam bounced and jiggled with joy. The two owls touched beaks again before Anam flew back out into the afternoon sun.

Above Coll Spring Anam looked down over Ferne Stone. *Kiew, kiew,* he called. Sion and Reanne Fox looked up, nudged muzzles together.

Wow! Wow! barked Sion as he watched Anam speed across the sky.

Daffodils lined up along the drystone wall and soft shades of heartsease coloured the north ridge. Bees buzzed between the flowers, and the sound of chippering grasshoppers celebrated spring's return.

High above the pine tops, Anam heard the cuckoos calling. Dipping down below the dark canopy, he saw Ailm Forest was restored, painted purple under a blanket of bluebells. In the far region of the wood, Anam heard two tawny owls marking the boundaries of their territories. *To-wit,* called the female. *To-woo,* the male replied. Anam flew low to the ground, dipping through the purpled woods. He observed a family of roe deer prick up their ears, raise their heads and turn their faces into the wind. Anam saw the badgers had returned and redeemed their sett. The soft crooning of pigeon and turtle-dove filled the forest and high up in the tallest tree sat Otus Long-Eared Owl, his home reclaimed among the stately pines. Otus gave the loudest HOO!, nodded and winked as Anam dashed by.

Over the ridge and down into the sun-washed valley, Anam followed the winding river. Passing over the rocky falls, up along the avenue of elms, he headed out towards the flowering meadowlands.

Cara and Feòrag Squirrel squeaked with delight, came leaping from bough to branch of the ancient oak. Dru peered silently from his cosy hollow. *Kiew, kiew*, called Anam, and on wings outstretched, the little owl crossed the vast azure and vanished into a veil of wispy cloud.

Looking in the rear-view mirror, Brigit Dannan bid a silent farewell to her life in the city. She read the sign to Nemeton, turned off the motorway, and switched on the radio. Vivaldi's 'Spring' played from the speakers.

The seven-year squeeze and crush of commuting—that daily mad dash for train, bus and cab to the next audition—was over. Her mind was clear; no more acting, no more role-playing, no more pretending. She had a real life, in a real world, with a man she really loved. Brigit wound down the window and let her hair blow wild in the wind.

The End, wrote Peter. The last page rolled off the platen.

Peter stood triumphant over the typewriter. He collected up his manuscript, moved over to the window, and opened the drapes.

Billowing clouds blazed red across the evening sky. On outspread wings, Fireun and Iolair Eagle soared high above the ridge, moving with great speed, turning a full circle over the rise. Round they came, first one, then the other, climbing the air, spiralling above the spire. To the heavens the birds ascended, gliding effortlessly until their wings almost touched.

In that old grey tower on the eastern rise, the brass bell tolled its sonorous tone while the weather-vane turned on the changing wind, reflecting the last rays of the setting sun.

Insights

CHARACTERS

ANAM LITTLE OWL

Anam is a little owl with a big heart. Stubborn and fearless, he is a courageous truth seeker. The name Anam is a Celtic word which means 'soul'. It derives from the words Anam Cara, meaning 'soul friend'.

ATHENE LITTLE OWL

A little owl (Athene noctua) also called the owl of Athena. Traditionally used as a symbol of knowledge and wisdom in Greek mythology.

BALORID

Balorid is a derivative of the name Balor found in Irish mythology. This mythological tyrant was the leader of the Fomorians; a group of malevolent supernatural beings. Balorid bears not an ounce of kindness or compassion but only a high sense of his own importance.

BOD OSPREY

Bod stands for Bards, Ovates, and Druids (BOD). These are the three noble classes of ancient Celts. A Bard is a storyteller, poet and musician. Ovates are diviners, prophets and philosophers. A Druid is a political advisor, moral teacher and keeper of natural knowledge.

BRÂN RAVEN

Brân means raven in Celtic languages and was the name of a pagan god in Welsh mythology. Brân pays homage to Edgar Allan Poe's The Raven.

BRIGIT DANNAN

Brigit is a down-to-earth, happy-go-lucky loving woman of Irish descent. She is of a half-forgotten time when we were all young and carefree. Always smiling, even in the face of adversity. Brigit or

Brigid appears in Irish mythology as a member of the Tuatha Dé Danann; a supernatural race who dwell in the Otherworld.

BROGAN BADGER
Stuck in his ways, and anti-social, Brogan is a solitary animal and keeps to himself. Brogh is the badger in the Cornish (Kernewek) language. The Irish word for badger is broc or brocc.

BRONWEN WEASEL
Bronwen is the Welsh word for the weasel. She can be belligerent when in the company of others and cares only for herself.

BRYCH THRUSH
Brych comes from the Welsh language and means mottled or speckled. Known for his great singing voice, Brych is a member of the dawn chorus.

BRYONY BADGER
This mother badger was named after the woodland plant Black Bryony because of her skill for creeping among the trees and bushes.

CARA SQUIRREL
Cara is a spritely red squirrel and is not afraid of

anything. She will risk life and limb to help restore peace back to Nemeton. She is vivacious, confident, independent, and has a heart of gold. The name Cara is a Celtic word which means 'friend.' It derives from the words Anam Cara, meaning 'soul friend'.

CARINA DUCK
Carina means pure or beloved. Misnamed Jemima by Brigit, this little duck was not amused.

CLOVER
Clover is the name of the carthorse in George Orwell's Animal Farm.

CONNIE RABBIT
Connie comes from cony and coney, which is another name for a rabbit in the Celtic language. Alas, Connie and her family were snatched away by the stealers.

CONNYN RABBIT
Connyn comes from the Irish Gaelic word coinín which means rabbit. In Scottish Gaelic the word is coinean. He is a widower and takes care of his kits

all by himself. Connyn is always seeking out a safer world in which to raise his family.

CRUIDÍN KINGFISHER
Cruidín in Irish means kingfisher. Rarely seen, this bird is usually glimpsed as a flash of blue light ... and then is gone.

DEARG
The character of Dearg comes from 'far darrig' or 'fear dearg' and is a faerie of Irish mythology. Fear dearg, means Red Man, and this particular case, Dearg always has blood on his hands. Also based on Dearg Due who is a vampire-like entity in Irish folklore. Dearg-due means 'red bloodsucker', a demon that seduces (traps) men (animals) and then drains them of their blood.

DOBRAN OTTER
Also a widower, Dobran finds it hard to forgive and forget for what happened to his lifelong partner. Dobran comes from the Gaelic word Dobhran which means otter. This elusive creature loves the riverbank and waterways.

DREEAN WREN

Wren in Irish is Dreoilín. This little bird is often referred to as the Druid Bird. Always a little late in attending the dawn chorus.

DRU BARN OWL

Dru comes from the word Druid. Druids were members of the learned class among the ancient Celts. They acted as priests, teachers, and judges for the people (animals). The name Druid comes from a Celtic word meaning 'knower of the oak tree'. Dru watches over the animal kingdom from his oak tree home and provides spiritual guidance for all living creatures.

DRUANTIA PHEASANT

In the Celtic language, Druantia means Queen of the Oak or Queen of the Druids.

EAYN LAMB

Eayn is a Gaelg (Manx) word for lamb. Curious, and with a spring in his step, this little lamb is ready to take on the whole wide world.

ELAN HARE

Elan means energy, speed, confidence and

enthusiasm. This hare was awarded the prestigious title for being the fastest in his drove. In Celtic folklore, the hare represents bright or shining, prosperity and good fortune.

FEANNAG CROW
Feannag is a Scottish Gaelic word for crow. Misunderstood, and often ostracised, the crow learns to keep within their clan. Birds of a feather flock together.

FENNING
Fenning comes from the word fen, which means bog or swamp. Anything that crawls out of a swamp is likely to be inhuman.

FEÒRAG SQUIRREL
Feòrag means squirrel in the Gàidhlig (Gaelic) language. He is a loyal partner who pursues his romantic ideals with true chivalry.

FIREUN
Fireun is the totem name given by the animals of Nemeton to represent Peter Goodhope. The eagle (Fireun, Iolair) is noted for wisdom in Celtic stories and represents keen sight and the knowledge of

magic. The animals believe that Fireun is the chosen one, here to help them see hidden spiritual truths and save them from nefarious poachers. Saviour-like qualities they bestow upon him.

GAVINA HAWK
The Scottish name Gavina means white hawk and is the medieval form of Gawain, one of the knights of the Round Table in Arthurian legend.

GRANDFATHER
He was a kind and gentle man and played a strong father figure in Peter's early years.

GRANDMOTHER
Independent, resourceful, lively and quick-witted, she is the quintessential grandmother that everyone loves.

GREYNOG HEDGEHOG
Greynog comes from the Scottish Gaelic word gràineag, meaning hedgehog. She is prickly on the outside but soft on the inside. Over-protective, and rather shy, she must learn to 'open up'.

HAZEL DORMOUSE
Hazel Dormouse is a generous little creature,

always sharing her food with others. She embraces change and is always up for a new adventure.

HOK FALCON

Hok actually means hawk in the Cornish (Kernewek) language. But this bird of prey so liked the name that he borrowed it from a neighbouring tribe!

IOLAIR

Iolair is Gaelic for eagle. Here it represents Brigit in spirit form flying with Fireun (Peter).

JEMIMA

This little duck is really called Carina but Brigit calls her Jemima (a homage to Beatrix Potter).

JJ JAROME

Although Jarome means sacred or holy, this antique dealer appears anything but. Like some of his artefacts, he is ruinous and further declines with age.

JONAS

Shaved head, ear piercings and a scarred lip, Jonas is nothing more than a land pirate acting as if he's God's gift to the world.

KASEK WOODPECKER

Kasek is a Cornish word for woodpecker. He keeps to the woods and is more heard than seen!

KEYRREY EWE

Keyrrey comes from the Celtic language of Gaelg (Manx) and means ewe or sheep. All Kerrey wants is to have her baby lamb lie down with her in green pastures and for them to sit beside the still waters.

LOSGANN FROG

From Scottish Gaelic comes the word losgann which means frog or toad. He is lord of the lake with an unfailing song he croaks every evening.

LUGH WOOD MOUSE

He may be the smallest, but he is the greatest of warriors. The name Lugh comes from a figure in Irish mythology as a member of the Tuatha Dé Danann (a group of supernatural beings). Lugh Wood Mouse is here portrayed as a kinsman redeemer. Steadfast, and ready to right some wrongs. In Irish mythology, Lugh is the grandson of the Fomorian tyrant Balor whom he opposes.

LÚNASA MOUSE

Lúnasa is the Modern Irish name for August and the Autumn quarter of the Celtic year; a time when the Celts celebrated Lugh the Celtic God. In Old Irish the name was Lugnasad—a combination of Lug (the god Lugh) and násad, meaning an assembly.

MCCABE

Overweight and addicted to beer, McCabe is a big fat low-ranking constable.

MERLYN BLACKBIRD

The name Merlyn comes from the mythical figure Merlin, prominently featured in the legend of King Arthur. He is another member of the dawn chorus.

MORGAN

The name and character of Morgan are taken from 'The Morrígan', a figure from Irish mythology that represents war and fate. Morgan is like a living scarecrow, and beneath his crooked hat, his hair sticks out like straw. If he only had a brain!

MORION

Impeccably dressed, pseudo-upper-class, he was

once well-respected but has crossed over to the wicked ways of man. Morion takes his name from 'The Fomorions'; a supernatural race in Irish mythology.

MR TOAD
A green 1958 Austen-Healey Sprite Mk 1. A small open sports car commonly known as 'Frogeye' because its headlights were prominently mounted on the bonnet. A homage to Kenneth Grahame's 'Wind in the Willows'.

MURIEL
Muriel is the name of the white goat in George Orwell's Animal Farm.

NATHAIR SNAKE
Nathair comes from Old Irish meaning snake. She has a cold heart and hides in the grass waiting for any unfortunate wayfarer to cross her path.

OLD TOD
A local gardener who's been around for decades. Tod is the common name for a male fox.

OSTARA RABBIT
The word Ostara (Eostre or Eastre) is a name

associated with the spring equinox in pagan cultures.

OTUS LONG-EARED OWL
Otus is a long-eared owl (Asio otus), known for his prominent ear tufts. This owl prefers to roost and nest within dense foliage. He is secretive, nocturnal, and superbly camouflaged. Highly adapted for silent flight and precision hunting.

PETER GOODHOPE
Peter is an illustrator of Otherworlds, inspired by Celtic and Irish mythology. He fully immerses himself in his work and lets the power of the imagination run wild. Peter's character was inspired by the works of the poet, William Wordsworth. A man deeply touched by the natural world.

POPPY
Poppy is a wildflower. Colourful makeup. Colourful hair. Colourful clothes. She is exuberant, funny and a loyal and trusted friend to Brigit. Poppy loves the theatre world's glitz and glamour and always hopes for that 'Starring' role.

REANNE FOX
Form of the Welsh name Rhiannon, which means 'great queen' or 'divine feminine'. Bringer of wisdom and rebirth.

RHEA PHEASANT
Rhea was known as the sister of Cronus (who was chief of the Titans and often associated with King Arthur sleeping in Avalon).

RUDHEK ROBIN
Rudhek is the Cornish word for robin. He is also a member of the dawn chorus. Chirpy, friendly, and quick to the wing.

SION FOX
The name Sion comes from the Irish word sionnach, which means red fox. Sion is a liminal creature. Bold and brave, curious and clever, he knows the woods and fields like no other.

SOFIA DEER
Sofia (Sophia) is the female personification of wisdom in Gnostic mythology. Also known as Gaia, Earth Wisdom, Mother Earth, or World Soul, she is the benevolent feminine nature of the world.

SPIÉR SKYLARK

Spiér comes from the Old English word spir, meaning stalk of grass. In full song, this cheerful little bird rises up from the meadowlands and climbs high into the sky.

TOM TITMOUSE

The term tom titmouse is commonly used as an alternate name for the blue tit, a small passerine bird in the family, Paridae.

PLACES

AILM FOREST

Ailm is the Irish name of the sixteenth letter of the Ogham alphabet. It represents the pine or fir tree.

ANNWYN MOUNTAIN

Annwyn is based around the words Annwn, Annwfn and Annwfyn and is the Otherworld in Welsh mythology.

AWEN RIVER

Awen is a Welsh, Cornish and Breton word that

means inspiration. Awen is the creative muse of artists such as writers or poets and may be described as a flowing energy that carries the spirit of creativity.

BEITH BARN
Beith is the Irish name of the first letter of the Ogham alphabet, meaning birch tree.

COLL SPRING
The Gaelic word for hazel is Coll. Coll Spring is based on Connla's Well in the Irish Celtic Otherworld. Also known as 'The Well of Wisdom', or 'The Well of Knowledge'. 'The hazel might be said to be the quintessential Celtic tree because of its legendary position at the heart of the Otherworld. Here, nine magic hazel trees hang over the Well of Wisdom and drop their purple nuts into the water... the hazel nuts cause bubbles of 'mystic inspiration' to form on the surface of the streams that flow down from the well...those that eat the nuts... gain poetic and prophetic powers.'
- Ross Nichols

'And when the sun sets dimmed in eve, and purple fills the air, I think the sacred hazel-tree is dropping berries there, From starry fruitage, waved aloft where Connla's Well o'erflows; For sure, the immortal waters run through every wind that blows.' (Excerpt from Connla's Well by George William Russell)

DAIR GROVE

Dair is the Irish name of the seventh letter of the Ogham alphabet. It means 'Oak'.

FERNE STONE

Based on the word Fearn, which is the Irish name of the third letter of the Ogham alphabet and represents the alder tree. Standing Stones are large upright stones placed in the ground. Where there are two or more upright megaliths supporting a large flat horizontal capstone, it is known as a dolmen.

GHOSTWOOD

A dark, foreboding place. Don't go in there!

HOPE HOUSE

Hope House is the residence of Peter Goodhope.

HOPE LAND

Hope Land is the estate of Hope House inherited by Peter Goodhope.

MUIN LANE

The word muin is the Irish name of the eleventh letter of the Ogham alphabet. It represents the blackberry.

NEMETON

Nemeton is based on the Celtic word 'nemeton'. It means a sacred place or sanctuary and is often interpreted as a sacred grove protected by druids. Nemeton is also based upon the idea of Utopia, a word used to describe a perfect imaginary world. Utopia can also mean 'no place' or 'nowhere'. Can a perfect world ever be realised?

SAILLE LAKE

Saille is the Irish name of the fourth letter of the Ogham alphabet, meaning willow tree.

STRAIF MANOR

Straif is the Irish name of the fourteenth letter of the Ogham alphabet and represents the blackthorn tree.

THE OTHERWORLD

In Celtic mythology, the Otherworld is sometimes described as a mystical realm of everlasting life or the home to Celtic deities. A place of great beauty, abundance and happiness. Upon seeing a magical mist, supernatural beings or unusual animals, you may be entering the Otherworld.

TINNE NOOK

Tinne is the Irish name of the eighth letter of the Ogham alphabet. It is associated with the holly tree.

TERMS

BEDFORD

The dilapidated vehicle is a Bedford CAS Mk 1 Canopy Pickup and has a distinctive pug-nose. It's seen better days!

BONEBREAKER

A metal foothold trap used by poachers for trapping animals.

CELTIC

The Celts were tribes of people who spoke their own Celtic languages, dating back to the Iron Age. There are six living Celtic languages: Breton, Irish, Scottish Gaelic, Welsh, Cornish and Manx.

DRYSTONE WALL

Dry stone walls are constructed from stones without the use of mortar to hold them in place. Often used for establishing the boundaries of fields.

KEYTOP

A mechanical typewriter 'keyboard'.

LANGUAGE OF THE ANCIENT EARTH

Nature is a living language, a divine natural language involving all the senses. A homage to The Prelude by William Wordsworth.

...'In storm and tempest, or in starlight nights
Beneath the quiet Heavens; and, at that time,
Have felt whate'er there is of power in sound
To breathe an elevated mood, by form
Or image unprofaned; and I would stand,
Beneath some rock, listening to sounds that are
The ghostly language of the ancient earth...'

LAPHROAIG

Laphroaig is a single-malt Scotch whisky named after Loch Laphroaig on the Isle of Islay.

MORRIS CAR

A 1961 Morris Minor Sedan. Looks like it's been dragged out from a nearby pond!

OGHAM

Ogham is an ancient alphabet used on wood and stone for inscribing messages, personal names and marks of land ownership found in fields and hilltops across Ireland, England, Scotland, Wales and the Isle of Man.

ORBIS ARBOUR

Orbis indicates the circle and means fulfilment. The Ancients referred to it as the Universe. An arbour is a sheltered place formed by trees and climbing plants and is often seen as an entrance into a garden. Here, Orbis Arbour is Nature's Gateway into the Otherworld.

PACKHORSE BRIDGE

Made from locally quarried stone, this arched

bridge was built for horses loaded with side-bags to take them across the stream.

REED BED
A natural habitat found in floodplains, lakes and estuaries.

SCALLY CAP
A flat cap with a small stiff brim in the front. Also known as a paddy cap in Ireland, as a bunnet in Scotland, and in Wales, a Dai cap.

STEALER
The Stealers are a misfit gang of poachers. There's no honour among these thieves!

THE BATTLE OF BALOR
A mythological tale about a group of malevolent supernatural beings led by Balor the 'Evil Eye'.

THUNDERFIRE
Shotguns used by poachers.

TREE OF LIFE
A metaphor found in many writings all over the world that symbolises the interconnectedness of everything.

VIVALDI

Antonio Vivaldi was a Venetian composer and violinist. The Four Seasons is a musical score which gives a musical expression to each season of the year.

Robin has wandered many ancient paths across England, Wales and the Outer Hebrides. Walking in nature has been the inspiration for all his writings.

Robin's first publishing success was *The Land of Ladybirds and Pirates*, which described his solo trek round the Cornish Coast, printed in the Cornish Scene magazine in 1985. In 2010, Robin received the WA Premier's Book Award for *The Garden* (Digital Narrative).

He lives with his wife on a small hobby farm in Western Australia and loves spending time in nature, tending to his three sheep and walking the dogs.

ALSO BY ROBIN CRAIG CLARK

The Garden: A Love Story for the Soul

Voyager: The Art of Pure Awareness

The Miracle of Flowers

Puri: Search for Paradise